INTRODUCTION.

An old tree stump is just a physical and visual reminder of an old tree that is no more. However, it can be a coffee table, a book rest, a seat, a bar and even a place of contemplation. When dry it is not raining, when wet it probably is or has been – just a tree stump.

Thursday is not a particularly important day, just one in seven. The Town of Sprockly is not a particularly important place and the good folk of this community would not generally suggest that they were exceptionally special in any way.

It is Thursday, rain is threatened, nothing new in that, families are going about their usual fourth day of the week routines, some of the men folk in the evening, will be getting together to play and watch their weekly darts match down at the pub, some friends are preparing for a coming wedding, a few youngsters are having disco in the back room of an inn. It is just a Thursday........ what can change the very ordinary and regular into something extra-ordinary?

1 A CAP AND A CAR

George Turnbull is a widower, well that is what he told everyone, in fact his wife had left him for the window cleaner after 25 years of marriage, they divorced shortly after she went. He moved to Sprockly about 7 years ago and very quickly fitted into the community and found himself a new partner in Shelley Howe (nee Sutcliffe) a widow of the town butcher, Jack Howe.

Her son, Paul Howe, still runs Howe's butcher's shop which is next to the Spar Store. Their relationship was an open secret to most in the town who knew them but they only moved in together a year ago, they are now due to get married at St Mary's on Saturday afternoon, the reception is being held in the back room of The Plough. George spent a good deal of time explaining the truth of his marital situation with the Vicar of St Mary's, Tom Wilson who assured him that all would be OK on the day

George is not showing his age, having just made 65 and collected his bus pass and state pension. George sadly never knew his father, he being killed early in World War 2 on one of the ill-conceived daylight bomber operations. He was brought up by his Mother and Grandmother in, Gorton, Manchester. They both worked to support the growing and developing George, his Grandmother dying at the ripe age of 84 and still missed. George's mother is in a nursing home on the north side of Sprockly, he brought her over to the town to ensure he could help her in her twilight years, Mrs Turnbull is as bright as a button but sadly her joints are not as they were. George took her out at least once a week in his purple Mondeo and visited regularly as did

Shelly.

George has a beard, that is not a beard, looking close to being un-shaven to scruffy, but he likes it and clearly Shelley is not making any changes until after the marriage. His hair and beard is all grey, he has a ruddy complexion, blue eyes and the kind of bulbous nose that suggests he likes his whisky, when in reality he rarely drank and when he did it was a shandy.

George's clothes were similar to his face, bordering on scruffy but clean. His clothes generally had seen better days, he always wore a cap, it has been suggested it had been given to him as a Christen-ing present as it was so distorted and worn, but he loved it, Shel-ley may change it in a little over a week's time. He like his brogue shoes, brown and corduroy trousers, heavy cotton shirts and at weekends always a tie.

Today he was without his tie as usual, his cap was on as he worked in his garden with Shelley watching him from her chair in their garden.

When they decided to move in together, they had two houses so to save possible arguments, they sold both and bought a new one, well not exactly new, a dorma-bungalow, built mostly of stone and about 120 years old. The whole building had been renovated by past owners and was in peak condition. George loved his gar-den and that is what he spends a good deal of time doing when not with his mum.

The potential beauty of the garden could be seen, the daffodils were dying off, the tulips were still blooming and the roses were starting to bud, all was coming alive.

"Want a brew love?", asked Shelley from the kitchen window, "yes please, my little wife-to-be and a bit of cake eh" replied George already putting down his hoe and looking at the dark clouds building up in the west. "Looks like rain" said George, Shelley did not reply she had already gone into the kitchen, but then waved through the small window at her love, and George waved back. They had a pine picnic table on their patio and George sat there waiting for his brew and looking at his garden with some pride. George looked at his Mondeo and noticed he had left his driver's door window open, so got up and closed it, not wanting to let the rain in. The clouds were getting thicker and darker, but it was still dry.

George loved his life, his new life, he loved Shelley and for him the future, even at his age looked good and fulfilling, the only thing he has insisted on since living with Shelly is that he would clean the windows himself, he totally trusted her, just did not like window-cleaners.

Shelly came out of the kitchen door carrying a tray, tea pot, milk jug, sugar bowl, two cups, two saucers, two tea spoons, two napkins and on a cake stand, far more pieces of cake a normal person could eat at one siting, but this was George and Shelley liked to do and have things done properly.

With a growing smile George, watched Shelley prepare this afternoon feast on their picnic table and just said "thank you", Shelly just smiled back. "Not doing much more, the weather is on the turn and besides, I need a bath before tea and then it is the match tonight" George was half way thorough his first piece of cake when he finished that sentence. "Totally forgot about it being Thursday and Darts Night, but you going out will give me more time to prepare the baking menu for the reception" said Shelly.

The Plough had agreed that Shelly could bring all the cakes and desserts for the wedding reception and as an accomplished baker she was enjoying the planning and indeed the baking. George was enjoying the samples. Shelley, via Paul was also supplying all the raw and cold meats for the reception, The Plough were doing the cooking and preparation and all helped to keep the cost down, George was not bothered he just wanted to get married, but Shelley being a businesswoman most of her life just like to make deals and she did.

"What's for tea love?" asked an always hungry George, "I was doing pork chops, mushrooms, peas, apple sauce and chips, how does that sound?" "bloody fantastic" said George, tucking into his third piece of cake and no tea had been poured yet. "I'll start the tea George, I trust you can pour your own tea" Shelley said as she disappeared through the kitchen door, George muttered something through a mouth full of cake, and then poured two cups of tea, milked and sugared both and took one into the kitchen for Shelley. "Thanks love, but next time, you will take your boots off, before coming into my kitchen", smiled Shelley, George doffed his cap with a smile and went back to his picnic table to view his garden.

"The clouds are getting darker love so I thought I would do you a favour and bring the tray in and save you getting wet", said George with a wide smile, Shelley just laughed and asked George to put the pots in the dishwasher, which he did after he gingerly stepped back to the door and removed his boots.

"60 positive replies to our reception George, I hope it does not go any higher, it should make for a great time without busting the bank", "that is great" said George with a tone that he tried to not show any indifference to the event as he was, not looking forward to the reception at all. The thought of having to give a speech just terrified him. He just wanted to get married and did not realise that Shelley would want to celebrate the day rather just have a Church service, but at least George would see his only child, James, his wife Ann and his two grandchildren Zoe and Walter who he had not seen in three years and who had not yet met Shelley. James had been living and working in Canada where he met his wife and brought up his children and the whole family was making a special trip to the UK arriving tomorrow at Heathrow, Shelley had prepared the spare attic rooms for them.

"Please mention to Paul when you see him tonight that The Plough want the meat I ordered, delivered latest tomorrow noon", "will do" said George as he read the news on the front page of the local paper that had just been delivered.

"Have I got time to run a bath before tea my love?", "of course you have" said Shelley as she peeled the potatoes for her chips.

George stripped down to his underwear and put his gardening clothes in the closet nearest the kitchen door, Shelley had designated that closet for such purposes and like a comic figure George disappeared towards the bathroom in his cap, baggy underpants, floppy socks and over large string vest. Shelley smiled with that loving expression of pure affection and got back to preparing tea. "Cap" came the cry from Shelley with a smile and George returned in all his sartorial elegance and put his cap on a hook on the back of the kitchen door and with a grin proceeded upstairs with underpants flapping.

The sky outside was getting darker thought Shelley, when the first clap of thunder shook the house. Shelley dropped her knife in the sink and hurried off to find George, she found him having a bubble bath with foam covering his head and clinging to his beard and quickly forgot her fear of thunder and just laughed and sat down on the bathroom stool.

"George that clap of thunder really frightened me, I never saw the lightning only heard the thunder", "storm must be miles away lass, that is why you did not see any lighting", with that the whole bathroom lit up with lightning outside followed almost immediately by a violent thunder clap that sent Shelly in her fear to fall into the bath, on top of George, again the fear went, they laughed kissed and laughed again. "This is new George, two of us in the bath" with a little difficulty she stood up, recognising her clothes were soaked through and not wanting to wet her bathroom floor she started to undress, wringing her clothes out over George's head and throwing them into the bathroom sink, when she was down to her underwear she sat down opposite George, which resulted in the bath overflowing and wetting her floor anyway. She laughed, he laughed the knickers came off as did the rest, tea would be a little later than planned.

George, ever the gentleman, let Shelley get out of the bath first and being ravenously hungry, suggested she just put on the bath robe to continue tea and that he would tidy up the bathroom and get dressed for the evening match. Shelley agreed, knowing full well that she would have to clear up the bathroom after George's efforts.

George heard the cry "teas up" while fastening his braces, the rest could wait he thought, I'll eat now.

George and Shelley, ate in the kitchen, the dining room was for dining, which in Shelley's eyes was when special guests are invited. The kitchen table was a reclaimed piece of furniture in a beautiful condition but still retaining its vintage by it colour, a pale blue, well-worn top and carefully turned legs. The chairs were all timber, purchased with the table and made a fitting centre to their large kitchen. Tea was on the table, each plate had two chops, one egg, a portion of mushrooms and peas, a load of chips and dollop of apple sauce together with two large breakfast cups of tea, with saucers of course. "You didn't mention eggs earlier my love", "I didn't expect a bath and things for two either; you need the energy" Shelley remarked with a smile and a slightly flushed face.

The rain was hammering down now, "I'm phoning the team I'll pick them all up and take them to The Nags Head; save them getting wet as I virtually need to pass them going into Sprockly", "you are a good man George Turnbull and I am proud to be marrying you in yes, in two days' time, cannot wait to be Mrs Turnbull" said Shelley smiling broadly. "Ah, but tonight, in honour of our wedding on Sunday, I have been nominated captain of the team, just for tonight mind, but I am dead chuffed". Shelley just thought "little things bring so much pleasure to my man, I am lucky, but he is a little daft".

George went to make his phone calls, still only partly dressed, but with a real spring in his step and a smile across his face that showed he was equally proud. His plate was clear; Shelley was only halfway through hers, but she was happy she had things to do while George was out; baking for her reception.

George came downstairs, dressed, sat down on the stool adjacent to the stairs, picked up the shoehorn which he kept on a nail under the stairs and put on his highly polished brogues, which were about the "only thing remotely smart", as Shelley often commented.

"You know, Harry is a real car snob, I am sure he did not want a lift in my purple monster, just because it smells a bit" said George while struggling with his shoehorn. "Never mind dear, you have all day tomorrow to get the car smelling beautiful, all vacuumed out and polished before the family arrive" said Shelley with a knowing smile, while George was just wanting his garden and a quiet wedding.

She had bought George a special suit for the wedding with new black brogues, a formal white shirt, suitable tie and matching pocket handkerchief, there would be no cap and there would be cuff-links she insisted.

George up from the stool and dressed for the darts, found Shelley, working through a mound of ingredients in a kitchen that was getting warmer by the minute as the two ovens were coming to temperature.

"I'm going now love, I will not forget to tell Paul about the meat, and I'll be picking him up first" said George holding his cap in his hand, "come here my little bubbles" said Shelley, George moved over slowly, still with cap in hand and got a face covered in flour as Shelley kissed him but first grabbed his head in both of her floury hands. "Have a great night, give my love to the team and tell them I expect to see them all on time, smart and tidy with their spouses at the Church on Saturday, oh and please tell them it is a wedding reception and not an opportunity for a rerun of tonight's match, so ask them to keep the darts at home". George turned to go, "love you my little bubbles, I could get into this two in a bath lark", said Shelley, "Love you to, see you later" said a slightly blushing George. "Darts?", asked Shelley, "in the glove box", George replied as he left Shelley with her baking. He left the house and drove off in the heavy rain in his purple Mondeo to pick up Harry, his first port of call.

"My car stinks", thought George as he drove off "and "I should have put that petrol can in the shed, rather than it being in the boot, it makes the car stink more than normal, but I am not stopping in this weather".

2 THE MAN FROM THE CITY

Harry married later in life being now 51 years old. He is a career minded man who had little time for female company, in his 20s and 30s save for a few romantic encounters on holiday and in the office. He worked in the City, being part of the Wealth Management Team at Savage and Strong International Bank. He made an excellent salary, supported by regular and for many observers, obscene bonuses. He was a very private person and liked to maintain a reputation for personal integrity and ethics. He had one obsession however and that was a car collection, he had 12, all housed in an architect designed garage complex at his house just outside Sprockly, his favourite is a 1968 Morgan Plus 8, his most extravagant is a 1973 Lamborghini Urraco Coupe and his most treasured vehicle is the very first car that he owned a 1973 MG MGB in British Racing Green. All his vehicles were in an immaculate condition being maintained by local dealers and regularly cleaned by John Hopper who did it for the love of it. Harry and John were part of the same pub darts team.

Harry married Sam 9 years ago, when she was 24, after a rather booze fuelled encounter at a company party. Sam had been Harry's personal assistant's, assistant and they had only exchanged the polite exchanges of "hello", "nice to see you", "how are you" and the like, he was focused on making money to buy cars and have a nice house in the country. However, that changed when Sam seduced him when he was somewhat worse for wear

after downing too many drinks which had been spiked by his se-
ducer. In a lockable photo-copier room she had her wicked way
with him and within 6 weeks confronted him with the news that
she was pregnant with his child. Sam even showed him a pregnancy testing kit's positive result as evidence.

Harry responded by proposing to Sam in a very hurried way,
they flew to Las Vegas and were married all within 2 days of her
announcement. Sam was happy more than happy and suddenly
very wealthy. The pregnancy ended with a fictitious miss-car-
riage, she maintained the false pregnancy by using kits that her
good friend Alice, who was pregnant, had used. Harry, as usual
was convinced by the evidence and as in all things responded ac-
cordingly.

As their time together was based on an initial falsehood the early
years were not that easy for either of them. Sam was given an
excellent monthly allowance by Harry but ended up a virtual
prisoner in their ever growing pile in Sprockly which she detested, she loved the City life and missed it. Harry initially used
Sam as a housekeeper, cook and the occasional sex companion.
She hated his cars, he disliked, as he saw it, the baseless vitality of
the City bright lights.

However, 4 years ago their dog Charlie died. They had purchased
their Golden Labrador puppy after a few months of marriage,
Harry thought it would be good company for Sam while he was
away from home on business. The dog became almost a substi-
tute child for both of them, they both loved him. Charlie developed cancer and although money was no object in trying to
save him, it proved to be futile. Charlie was put to sleep by the
vet with both Sam and Harry holding him and holding back their
respective tears not wanting their beloved child to sense their
emotions.

They had left the vets in silence, climbed into Harry's Range
Rover and driving home not talking. They entered their house
in silence, they both went into the kitchen and Sam put the ket-

tle on, all was quiet. Harry sat down on his kitchen stool and the whole thing become too much for him and he started to sob; sob loudly with torrents of tears. Sam, putting down two mugs on the work surface, also began to cry and cry with real emotion to such an extent her whole body shook and her tears started to wash away her makeup. She moved over to Harry and just grasped him from behind, resting her head on his left shoulder and they cried together. After a short while, Harry turned his head to Sam and Sam adjusted her stance to turn hers to his and they kissed, not a word had been said since Charlie's demise, but they kissed and kissed and kissed again. They kissed like they had never done in their whole relationship.

Sam grasped Harry's hand and while both of them were still crying tears of loss, she led him to their bedroom, upstairs and they made love like they had never done before. Love had found them both through this loss of their dog, this loss of Charlie.

From that encounter or from one of many shortly after Sam became really pregnant and they were both over the moon.

Their son David is just 3 now and going through the nightmare of tantrums linked to the 'terrible threes' although there was also the 'terrible twos'. Fortunately, there is a superb nursery school in Sprockly and David is there from 9.30 in the morning till 4.00 in the afternoon, Monday to Friday, Sam wishes it was every day.

As usual Harry was in the City, but would be on the earlier train to get back in time for his weekly night out. Sam was waiting for Paul her 'supplier of sausage'. She has been having an off, on, relationship with Paul for just over a year, their ages were very close and she liked his flirty and natural flamboyance, she also thought he was pretty good in bed as well. There was no love there, she just like sex with a handsome man and she kept the whole relationship very hidden indeed.

It was looking like rain as Paul Howes', Range Rover pulled up at the grand house of Harry and Sam to deliver his Pork and Apple

Sausages.

Paul rang the bell with his wicker basket under his arm. The door opened and Paul went in and put his basket down and grabbed Sam around the waist, "your delivery madam". Sam did not say a word as Paul led her towards the large family room and said "stand still" in a very demanding way. Sam did just that and Paul just started to undress her. In less than a minute she was naked and in less than a further 15 seconds so was Paul. Not a word was said as they made love on the couch, nor was a kiss hardly shared, all that mattered to both of the combatants was a sexual encounter. After they had both got what they wanted, Paul got up and went to the toilet just off the family room washed himself and came back and got dressed. Sam in the meantime was dressed and tidying up the couch's covers and cushions. "your later than normal Paul", "yes sorry" said Paul putting on his clothes, "I was delayed by having to prep all the meat for George and Shelly's wedding, I knew Harry would be home soon, so sorry about the rush". Sex with Paul was always a rush, but she did not mind, she got out of it what she wanted as Harry was less demanding or able these days, which she put down to his age.

"Thanks for the sausages, put them on my bill and I'll send you my next order tomorrow for the weekend", Paul was now dressed and leaving the door with his empty wicker basket under his arm, he smiled and closed the door. By now the clouds were thickening and the rain was heavy. Paul climbed into his Range Rover and roared off to his home.

Sam went upstairs, showered and got herself ready to pick David up from the nursery. On the way back from the nursery David had fallen asleep in the car, so on arrival home, Sam carefully lifted him off his booster seat, closed the car with barely a clink, carried the sleeping 3-year-old time bomb into the house and into the downstairs nursery, placing him snuggly into his bed.

Just as she closed the nursery door the biggest clap of thunder happened, Sam was shocked by the noise and immediately re-opened the door to check on David, who was still fast asleep, thumb firmly fixed in his mouth, with regular sucking sounds being made, smiling gently Sam closed the door after blowing a kiss.

Sam breathed a sigh of relief and went into the kitchen to prepare dinner for Harry, David and her; using Howes' famous Pork and Apple sausages.

The rain was getting heavier outside as Sam stood at the kitchen prep sink, carefully peeling potatoes, washing them as she went and placing the peeled spuds in a bowl of cold water.

The telephone rang, drying her hands she picked up the kitchen phone from the wall mounting, it was Paul. She finished the phone call as Harry's Jaguar XK Coupe pulled into the drive with the words "shit, shit shit".

Harry opened the large front door, dropping his brief case as he usually did behind the umbrella stand, took his coat off, shaking it briefly outside to remove what little rain had fallen on it and hung it in the closet, "shush" said Sam, "David is asleep and he slept through an enormous clap of thunder, so he must be tired", Harry leaned forward placed his finger across his lips, smiled and then gave Sam a kiss on the cheek.

"Sam, we need to talk", "OK let's go into the kitchen" said Sam, looking somewhat perplexed, as Harry was not renowned for his domestic chat.

"Coffee?" said Sam, "not just yet, a scotch would be more appropriate, but to the point, if you don't mind, this is delicate and for me something rather embarrassing". Harry paused and just looked at the kitchen floor, before continuing "you know I love you and only you" said Harry now looking at Sam's breasts rather than her face. "I'm all ears love", said Sam, now really puzzled and a little frightened about what was coming. "Sam, oh God this hard for me, so just let me speak and ask questions when I have finished", "OK" said Sam now even more nervous about what Harry was going to say.

"Sam, I've been going to see a Doctor in the City", Sam, grabbed a tea towel and put it too her mouth, tears were already welling up in her eyes, "no, no nothing life threatening Sam, nothing serious, you spoke without speaking", the tea towel stayed across her mouth. "Sam, you know things have not been good for us in the bedroom, Oh God, this is difficult" said a now blushing Harry, he went on "well I went to the Doctor and asked for his guidance and help", Sam just sat there, tea towel now in her mouth, eyes very wide open wondering what was coming next. "I've had tests and further tests and it would appear what is wrong with me is not uncommon with men of my age and it can be beaten, I even got tested for prostate problems and all is clear".

All through this one-sided conversation Harry had been looking at the floor and Sam's breasts and now he lifted his eyes to meet Sam's eyes, "I need some hormone replacement treatment, a bit like women do during the menopause and also a little blue tablet that appears to act like spinach did to Popeye". "There how do you feel Sam?", "I have not got a clue what you are talking about Harry" said Sam, having removed the kitchen towel from her mouth "and who is Popeye?". "Sorry Sam, it has been embarrassing, frustrating and humiliating, I have not been able to perform in the bedroom, because literally I could not make love to you even though I desperately wanted to", "well I guessed that", said Sam "you often started what you could not finish", "well hopefully all that is over with, with the replacement hormone stuff and little blue tablets you had better watch out" Harry said with a beaming smile, Sam smiled back "what blue tablets and you still have not told me about Popeye?" Harry got off his kitchen stool and went to the hall to recover his brief case.

He put the brief case on the kitchen island unit, opened it and recovered to two paper prescription bags. The first one he opened was his medication, the second contained Viagra slides which he passed to Sam. "Oh I've read about these, these, these tablets in magazines" said Sam with a tone of excitement resulting in a slight unbecoming stutter and wonder, hardly able to get her words out, "cost a bit" said Harry "but if they work, yabadaba-doo!", "don't care how much they cost, if they work" said a very smiling Sam.   Harry's embarrassment over, he now was just sweating with relief, "so who was Popeye?", said a still quizzical Sam, "Popeye was a black and white cartoon sailor-man who gained superhuman strength by eating spinach, so Viagra, it may be blue, but it is pure spinach to this man." said Harry with a casual air pointing at himself.

"How long does it take to work, is it immediate?" said Sam, "in about an hour, so I have been told, not much spontaneity but I guess a good deal of expectation" said Harry in a knowledgeable tone, "the medication is daily and probably for life, the little blue bombs of spinach are for as and when", "so when is the next as and when?" asked Sam with little blush on her face, "how about in an hour's time" Sam suggested, answering her own question and already feeling somewhat aroused, "how about later when I get back from the pub and I promise I'll be drinking shandy all night, don't want to spoil the moment".   "You're on" said Sam, with a real smile and now a spring in her step as she went back to preparing dinner. Sam was wondering what to wear to further titillate the coming night's pleasure as Harry went upstairs to shower and change, but before he went, he checked on David, who was still sucking his thumb and fast asleep.

The rain was still pouring down and the late spring sky was getting darker as further clouds gathered.

When Harry came down in his 'pub gear' he found David just awake sat in his special high chair, at the kitchen dining table, Sam had turned the radio on to BBC Radio 5 live, which suited Harry as he disliked modern music and like the non-stop news format, whereas Sam just put up with it and David was simply used to it, not understanding anything really.

Harry sat down in his short sleeved 'dart's' shirt, displaying sponsorship brands he had never heard of, but he had to wear a shirt like the professionals, even though he was pretty useless and his red jeans which he loved and Sam hated. "One day those trousers will be in the bin", thought Sam, "but then he would just go out and buy another pair so there would be no point really", Sam just smiled with a slight shake of the head.

Sam delivered her meal a bowl of cut up sausage, mash and a little cider gravy for David, a plate for herself of reasonable portion size and a mountain for Harry, he just loved this meal. "Forgotten something" said Harry, "oh my, oh my" said Sam, sounding a little breathless rushing to the oven and producing some piping hot Yorkshire Puddings, "my mistake, those little blue tablets of spinach are affecting my mental processes and I am not taking them, let us hope your libido is similarly affected", Sam said with a smile, David had already put most of his meal on the place mat and was happily playing with the sausages with car sounds. Harry just laughed, still slightly embarrassed that the conversation was still on spinach.

As they finished their meal with Harry recounting some Doctor things to Sam, David asked for 'toilet', so Sam picked him up and took him to the loo, just off the family room. Paul had been the last person in there and she quickly tidied the room while David did what he needed to do.

Sam heard the phone go, Harry picked it up, "Hi George, what's up?" said Harry, "oh that is very kind of you, I can do the picking up if you want George", "oh ok if you insist, look forward to seeing you and thanks a lot George, you must tell me how the planning is going for the big day on Saturday, see you in a bit". "Damn" said Harry nearly slamming the phone down, "I know he means well, but George is picking us all up, to go to the Nag's for our match tonight, as the weather is so bad, his car is a moving wreck and smells, oh boy does it smell, I don't know how he makes a car smell like that", "Stop moaning and be grateful", said Sam with a smile and holding David's hand. "David is going to have a thirty-minute play in his nursery and then I'll read him a book, hopefully to sleep for the night", "oh please let him sleep tonight, I want no visitors to our bedroom at 11 o'clock like last night" thought Sam, the same thought was also going through Harry's mind.

Sam took David to his nursery and Harry picked up the local newspaper to what was not happening in the Sprockly area.

"Have you got your darts?", asked Sam, "rats" exclaimed Harry as he dropped the paper on the kitchen table and proceeded to his study. He always kept his darts in his left hand draw of his desk, next to his walnut case containing the keys for his special cars, that is how much he prized his darts and his evening of being normal with the 'lads'.

He returned to the kitchen table, darts secure in his shirt breast pocket, just like a professional, without the beer belly. He continued to read where he had left off, why he looked at the classified bewildered Sam as he never bought anything from them, but it nevertheless fascinated him.

"Harry I've been thinking about holidays, David is getting old enough to fly now and perhaps we could think about going to somewhere, not too hot, but somewhere other than car shows or events, what do you think?" Harry put down his newspaper, smiled, left the kitchen table and went to his briefcase by the door and behind the coat stand. From his briefcase he produced a collection of travel brochures and proudly dropped them on the kitchen table with a "there you go, or should I say, there we go". "You are brilliant", said Sam, with a beaming smile, as she started to review what had suddenly fallen on the table. Harry returned to the classifieds while Sam rummaged through the various brochures with her smile reducing to a facial frown. "Harry" she said in a less than happy tone, "these brochures are all foreign car events, I just wanted a normal family holiday", she emphasised 'normal'. Harry put down his newspaper, smiled at Sam and went again to his brief case, returning with another collection of holiday brochures with the comment "only having you on darling, I was thinking on exactly the same while leaving the office today, so I called into a travel agency before getting the tube, sorry about the others, my humour I am afraid". Sam picked up the car related brochures and dropped them into the recycle bin while returning to the table and kissing Harry head after pushing his paper to one side. She studied the brochures while Harry continued to review the classified.

Harry broke the silence, Radio 5 Live was still playing, by telling Sam, "wherever you want to go, we would go, along with Popeye's spinach". Harry smiled and went back to his newspaper, Sam got a notebook and pen from the kitchen draw and started to review the brochures.

Time passed, the radio playing, David still asleep, brochures and classifieds being scrutinised. Harry heard George's car in the drive, he dived for the door, not wanting the door chimes to awaken David. He just made it opening the door just as George was about to push the button. "Just in time" said Harry, stooping rather comically as he opened the door, to a rather surprised George, "didn't want to wake up David, George", "oh fully understand Harry, you should try and get door chimes that don't wake the dead", George replied with a smile. "A second" said Harry, as he dashed inside the house and headed towards the nursery. He opened the door quietly and looking inside finding David fast asleep, thumb in mouth as always, all tucked into his bed with Sam equally asleep in her chair with her nursery story book on her lap. He slowly kissed his index finger and gingerly placed it on David's forehead, smiled in his fatherly joy and then kissed Sam very gently on top of her head, she awoke slightly, smiled, opened her eyes gently, grabbed his shirt and kissed him properly, Harry's darts fell out of his shirt pocket, hitting one of David's toys on the way down, which stated the thing to make music, which in turn awoke David. "I'm out of here" said Harry as he blew a kiss to Sam and closed the door very gently but knowing that the damage had been done.

Harry was the first of George's pick-ups that evening as he jumped into the front passenger seat and the car still stunk, but given the weather it was not appropriate to open the windows but rely on the car's smelly ventilation system, 'oh that smell of car is tonight being masked by a smell of petrol', being a gentleman he refrained from mentioning the smell, just started with "evening George" to which George replied "evening Harry, how was your day?" as he drove off the rather splendid driveway of the house.

3 SAUSAGES

Paul Howe is the owner and proprietor of 'Howe's the Butchers of Sprockly'. The shop is situated next door to the Spar Store. Paul inherited the business on the death of his father seven years ago and pays his mum a small peppercorn rent for the premises which she still owns following the death of her husband, Jack.

Paul married Toni, his wife in 1996 and have one child a son called Jack, named after Paul's father and are expecting another child towards the end of May although Toni is already displaying a rather big tum, all tests have confirmed that it is only one baby, so it could be big one.

Paul and Toni, live in Paul's family house which he bought at well below market price from his mum, Shelley when she sold her home to move in with George. They lived in the property immediately after getting married as they could not afford a mortgage at the time, Paul's mum was happy to live in a room within the house. However, as the house had 5 bedrooms, three bathrooms and plenty of reception rooms it was no real hardship.

'Howe's the Butchers of Sprockly' is a growing business, through careful planning and marketing Paul has developed a real reputation for quality meats and delivers to over 20 restaurants and pubs in the area and has since 2003 had to employ a delivery driver full time, who also helps out in the shop when needed. Things are looking good.

All is not well with Paul and Toni, Paul is convinced the baby Toni is carrying is not his and at the same Paul is having an affair with

Sam, the wife of one his friends, Harry. Toni on the other hand knows full well that the baby is Paul's but thinks that her husband is having an affair with his delivery driver's wife Pam, which he is not, although at a Christmas party he did try it on a bit, which Toni saw and put 2 and 2 together and got 3.

Despite his infidelity Paul, dotes on his son Jack and is fearful that if it ever came out in the open, he would lose contact with the one person he really truly loves.

Paul likes to play the old fashioned butcher, wearing aprons like Corporal Jones and wearing a straw boater hat complete with a ribbon that mirrors the shop logo colours of purple and gold. His shop is spotless and bears the proud symbols of hygiene window posters that the local authority like to issue from time to time. He prices his meat in imperial measures and displays the metric measure equivalent in similar sized characters on his pricing boards, he says his customers prefer proper weights, although local trading standards have warned him about it, he just dislikes the European Union and all it interferes in.

Paul is getting ready to close up, he closes early on Thursdays so that he and Bob the delivery driver can do their individual deliveries to business and private customers prior to the shop weekend rush, which starts on Friday, with early morning deliveries which will need preparing.

Bob has noticed that Paul only takes one or two deliveries while he will have up to 20 and in some circumstances 30 to make on a Thursday afternoon and evening. Today was no different.

"See you tomorrow Bob, safe journey, give me a call on the mobile when you have finished" said Tony, "OK Tony, see you tomorrow, good evening", "strange reference to evening", thought Bob, it was mid-afternoon. "Bob, nearly forgot, first thing will you prep that meat for my mum's reception, the requirements are in the order diary and take them around to The Plough as soon as?", "will do Paul, cheers".

Bob drives off in the purple and gold liveried refrigerated delivery van and Paul drives off in his personal British Racing Green Range Rover with a refrigerator in the back for his deliveries.

Paul noticed as he drove off that the clouds were getting darker and sensed that rain was in the air.

The Range Rover pulled up outside a house grander than Paul's, this was the home of Harry and Sam Easton. A recently constructed architect designed private, one off property, boasting 6 bedrooms, as many bathrooms, 4 reception rooms, two nurseries a games room, stables, a garage complex for goodness who knows how many cars, a swimming pool, you name it the house had it, but that is not all it had.

Sam and Paul have been seeing each other for the last 12 months usually when Harry was down in the City as he was most days. Sam had confirmed to Paul that Harry was still in London by phone just before the shop closed so he was making his delivery. It could not be a long liaison as Harry was in the darts team and always caught an early train to get home for dinner prior to going to the pub. Harry liked Howe's pork and apple sausages and that was what was being delivered for dinner, Sam preferred hers to be plain pork. Paul hid this relationship very well from everyone.

Paul parked up on his drive to be greeted by a bounding Jack and their ever loving border collie Tom. He picked Jack up with Tom bouncing around his heels and went through the front door. Toni was not having a good day, let alone her suspicions, she was feeling particularly tired and uncomfortable, the coming storm was not helping her mood either.

A clap of thunder shook the house, Tom tried to dive under the couch, Jack started crying, Toni looked genuinely frightened and Paul literally jumped not expecting anything. "Crickey that was loud and so unexpected, I did not see any lightning flash" said a startled Paul, "neither did this pregnant lump of fear you see before you" said Toni still shaking and at the same time trying to pacify a crying Jack, Paul went looking for Tom. The whole interior of their main reception room and conservatory lit up with a lightning strike followed almost immediately by a clap of thunder that would have stirred the dead, Tom was nowhere to be found, Jack was sobbing, Toni was really frightened, Paul was somewhat shocked and it was pouring down outside. "That was some bang, eh Jack, come here and we will look at the rain and clouds move away", Jack remained cuddling up to his mum still sobbing, Tom still could not be found. Paul just could not physically comfort Toni, and she desperately needed some reassurance, none was coming.

After a while, peace was restored, Tom appeared from goodness knows where and curled up on his cushion.

"Paul", said Toni, "you have a private and personal letter from the States, I left in the study, your usual mail is where it always is". "Ok", said Paul in a rather curt way and off he went to the Study, Tom, appearing from goodness knows where, now following him at his heel.

Paul opened the study door quickly and aggressively, closed it quietly while scanning his desk and then slowed almost to standstill when he saw the envelope perched up against the picture of his dad which he kept on his desk. It was from the private DNA lab.

A few months ago, following a flaming row between Paul and Toni, outside the earshot of Jack, Toni had agreed to have a pre-birth DNA tests undertaken on her unborn baby. This commercially available test had to be undertaken in the US at some expense but Paul was not bothered about the cost. That test would settle the argument once and for all. His eyes never left the envelope, he just slowly, very slowly walked around his desk and sat down, took a deep breath, closed his eyes for a moment and reached for the letter opener. Paul was not a nervous man, but now his hands were really shaking, he checked that the envelope had not been tampered with, it had not been. He could hardly get the knife into the envelope flap, finally he succeeded and it opened with that reassuring quiet but good cutting sound. He removed the letter, only one piece of American equivalent A4 headed paper appeared, he very rapidly scanned the initial blurb and Paul went directly to the summary, Toni's baby was his.

Paul dropped the letter opener and put the letter gently on his blotting pad and he just looked forward, looking at nothing, he started to cry. He simply did not know what to do, he was a stubborn man, not noted for accepting fault or being wrong. He liked balance, if he did something wrong, everybody else also did things wrong, it was a strange balancing act that he saw in life and relationships. He always wanted the baby to be his and yet somehow, because of his own infidelity he could not believe that Toni could be faithful and yet in reality he still loved her with his very being and this was the shock to the system so badly needed for him and the future of his family.

Paul had a small toilet off his study and he went there to freshen up his face, looking at the mirror, he inwardly said "you bloody, bloody, bloody idiot!" He couldn't stop the tears; he had not cried in years, he was a proud and stubborn man, he was being hit by this news in two ways that emotionally he found more than difficult, firstly that he was wrong, when in his reality he was never wrong, it was him that was the adulterer, he had nearly wrecked all he loved and cared for and secondly he was to be a father again and he loved and cherished that responsibility.

With Tom still at his heal he left the Study and went to the family room where he had left Toni and Jack. He found them still curled up together on the couch, Jack was nearly asleep and Toni was dozing as well. "Toni, Toni", Paul said with a quiet warm tone that he had not used for months, "Toni can we talk, I'll take Jack to the nursery he can sleep there, while we talk", still using a quiet, close to sobbing soft tone of speech, Paul gently picked up Jack, Tom at his heels and walked to the nursery which was just next to the family room and laid Jack into his low bed, covered him up, placed his favourite teddy in his arms, gave him a kiss and left the door slightly ajar so as not to startle Jack when he awoke. The nursery had started life as a big broom cupboard, but was converted and decorated as a nursery on the arrival of Jack so that he had a safe space down stairs, a luxury idea he had picked up from Sam and Harry following a visit to their house a few years ago.

As Paul left the nursery Tom stopped following and curled up in front of the door as if on guard which was one of his many loving ways of protecting the family. Paul went back to Toni.

Toni was sat on the couch her knees as best they could be brought up to a chest with a cushion between and her face in the cushion. "Toni, are you comfortable, as I am not, I do not know what to say or how to say it in trying undo all the nasty, horrible, nasty, terrible, hasty, bloody awful things I have said to you", croaked, a close to sobbing, Paul, hardly being able to get his word out, as tears poured to match the rain that was by now hammering out-side. Toni raised her face, she too was crying, but hers were heavy tears too, the cushion was wet, her make-up was in tatters and she reached out for Paul's hand and holding it placed it on her very large tummy, "Our baby Paul, all ours", Paul sat next to Toni, hand still on her tummy, kissed Toni for the first time in months and they both sobbed in each other's arms, Jack suddenly appeared with Tom following. Seeing the tears in mum and dad's eyes Jack rushed to the coffee table, pulled some tissues from the box and rushed back to his mum and dad giving them both a tissue with a "there, there", it broke the ice, they both smiled, they both laughed, the family was back together, Tom just stood there with a wagging tail. Paul felt the baby move, which did nothing for his tears.

Paul had not mentioned to anyone that Toni was pregnant, the immediate family was totally ignorant of the fact. Toni had fol-lowed Paul's instructions in not telling any friends or family, but she had spoken to the Vicar for advice as she thought her marriage was over, now it clearly was not.

"Toni, I'm just popping into the study" said Paul drying his eyes, "back in a mo, just need to collect myself". "Tea will be on the table in five", said Toni getting off her stool and stroking both Jack and Tom.

"I'm going to be a dad again", thought Paul getting up from the couch with wet tissue in hand, the shock suddenly hit him, in his strange denial he had made no plans and now suddenly he had to get his self in order in a month rather than the 8 months' notice you normally get. Paul was a stubborn man and when he made personal or public vows he held to them no matter what pain it causes, he collected himself went to the study, closed door, went around the desk sat down and called Sam.

Sam answered with her usual "hello, Sam and Harry's", "Hi Sam, it's Paul, Sam, I'll get to the point" Paul was speaking like a machinegun, "I know this is going to be hurtful, but I want our relationship to cease for the sake of your family and mine, we can still be friends but the sex stuff now stops for ever..... there was a silence then "the baby is yours after all" said Sam in a rather calmer voice than he was expecting, "yes" said Paul very quickly, "you are a shit, Paul Howes and I will always like your sausages" Sam responded very calmly "You are probably right our times were putting so much pressure on me, I did not like cheating on Harry, the fun had gone, the passion and lust went months ago, the sex was mechanical but I hoped in the latter months it helped you with your doubts in Toni while giving me something that Harry's does not for whatever reason want, sex with me" there was a silence, Sam kept going "Paul, I am so really pleased for you and Toni, oh", looking out of the window she saw Harry's Jag, "Harry's car's just pulled up" she continued "must go now, see you around you shit, shit, shit" the phone went dead, Paul breathed a sigh of relief and another tear filled up in the left eye and then the right and he sobbed and sobbed again into what was left of a very soggy tissue.

He heard the shout, "tea's ready", so he went to the toilet again washed his face and hands, looked into the mirror and saw a face with worries lifted, new worries applied and one looking towards a new life. Paul entered the dining kitchen, Jack was on his high stool, fork and knife in hand looking at an as yet empty bowl, two plates were set, Tom had his head in his bowl and a large Pyrex bowl sat in the middle of the table on a table mat, containing a steaming cottage pie which Toni had been cooking most of the afternoon, it was Paul's favourite before a drink in the pub, he reckoned it lined the stomach. Paul sat down in his usual chair and Toni with a still shaking hand give him a serving spoon to dispense the pie, Paul's hand was also shaking, Jack's was first, but then he was told "too hot just yet Jack" by a still shaking Paul, "so just wait a minute while it cools". Toni sat to table still with her apron on, her face was cleared of makeup and she looked radiant thought Paul, he served her next then himself. Then he got up went to the cupboard and produced his beloved HP sauce which he just loved in about anything and proceeded to smoother his steaming mound of pie.

The rain was still coming down outside but not as heavy as earlier, Toni was finding it difficult to find something to say after the recent emotional trauma and equally Paul just did not know what to say, so Jack piped, "am I really going to be a page boy at the wedding of Nan on Saturday, what page boys do, do I turn pages?", they both laughed, but to be fair it was a reasonable question from a 4 year old boy, "no pages to turn", Toni said, "just look nice in the very special suit that has been bought for you and walk with the bridesmaids, all of whom you know", "will there be jelly, cakes, ice cream, sweets and", "there will be everything a little boy like you likes at the reception", Toni interjected, "and Nan is making most of the cakes so you know how good they will be" said Paul, Jack had now gone off subject and was demolishing his bowl of cottage pie.

"After all that has happened today, I think it better I give the chaps a no for this evening" said Paul, "no way, Paul", said Toni, "the sooner we get back to normal the better, I have things to prepare for Saturday, like ensuring Jack's clothes are all pressed and tidy, that your formal shirt is pressed and hung and my clothes are right for the day, no I have enough to do without you hanging around. This time of the year Thursday is darts night, and you have something to share with your mates, you are going to be a dad again. Paul had kept Toni virtually out of sight of the circle of friends once the pregnancy became visually obvious, now was the time to tell and celebrate.

Tea was finished, Toni cleared up, Paul took Jack back into the family room with Tom in tow and all three sat on the couch to watch the six o'clock news.

The phone rang, Toni, now with even more tears coming down her face, picked up the phone, "hi Toni here", "hi Toni it is George", "everything OK?" asked Toni, half expecting the world to have had the same traumatic emotional experience she had just had. She wiped her eyes with a kitchen towel and George continued "everything is fine, firstly, I am instructed to please remind Paul about the meat to be delivered to The Plough tomorrow, also and probably more important, please tell Paul I will pick him up for the match tonight, the weather is foul, no point in us all getting wet", "we only live a stone's throw from The Plough, it is hardly worth it George" exclaimed Toni, "we are away tonight at The Nags Head", said George, "oh I see" said Toni, "I'll tell him, he would have probably gone to The Plough without thinking, thanks George, love to Nan" the sound of a kiss was made to the phone, "see you George if not before, in St Mary's on Saturday, bye" Toni put the phone done, wiped her eyes and went to join the family.

"Paul, George is picking you up", "but", was as much as Paul could say, "you are playing at The Nags Head tonight and the weather is not nice and don't forget your mother's meat for The Plough tomorrow". "The meat is in hand, Bob is sorting that, but I would still prefer to be with you this evening' said Paul, "not a hope, go out and enjoy yourself and think of the cuddles tonight, something I have missed for months", said Toni, Paul smiled with an apologetic look and turned to give a kiss to Jack who was now asleep, which prompted Tom to put his head on Paul's knee and demand a similar act of affection.

After a while Paul went upstairs to get showered and changed and just as he was coming back downstairs, the honk of George's car was heard on the drive outside. "Must go darling" said Paul, he had not used 'darling' for months, Toni left Jack asleep on the couch and Tom kept guard, to give Paul a kiss before he left the house as he turned before leaving he mouthed "I love you" with tears in his eyes, Toni was similarly crying, the evening had been traumatic but beautiful, Paul closed the door quietly after picking up his mac from the coat stand. Then Paul reappeared, grabbing Toni's hand he pulled her to himself, bent down and kissed the bump, raised his head kissed Toni again and left without saying a word.

Toni just stood there, both hands gently resting on her large tum, she could feel baby moving and loved it, and began to think that her feelings of Paul having an affair were about as irrational as his about her, Paul was a flirt, but that to some extend is a virtue rather than a negative. Paul looked so reconciled to our family she thought, Paul uncovered the love he always had, Toni, now mentally threw away her doubts, cried again and went back to Jack who was now awake and who rushed to get another tissue for his mum.

Paul dashed out, while pulling his raincoat on, he just got to the car and then dashed back to the house, "forgot my darts" he shouted as he ran to his study, grabbed the darts, that he had already left out, next to a very soggy tissue and hurried back out of the house, stopping briefly to give Toni another kiss, pat her tummy, smile at Jack who was now holding the box of tissues, stroked Tom's head and then into George's waiting car with Harry already sitting in the front seat. Paul dived into the back, but still got very wet, "sorry about that, nearly forgot my darts" said a Paul wiping rain spots off his glasses.

"Boy your car stinks" said Paul while brushing rain from his hair with his hands. "Evening Paul", said George, "Evening Harry", said Paul. The car drove off to pick up John.

4 THE HOUSE FROM SWEDEN

John had taken the afternoon off from his work. He had planned it for weeks and just hoped the weather would be kind and it was at the moment, but clouds were on the horizon. His overalls on, he was 'playing', as his wife, Judy called it, with his 1967 Austin Mini, which was his pride and joy. John was no mechanic, he just loved this car, its colour, its unreliability, its character and driving it. Judy looked out from her kitchen window, as she prepared tea and just wondered, as she always did, what on earth he was getting so much pleasure out of.

John worked in a local warehouse as fork-lift driver and load sorter, he loved the job, little responsibility, good pay, as the over-time was regular and it was local. His day car is a 2001 red Honda Civic, he thought the car was just about OK, but characterless and so reliable, he could not 'play' with it, however in reality he could do little under the bonnet, save for topping up water and checking tyre pressures.

John and Judy had been married since 1984, they both met at College, Judy was taking a secretarial course and John was taking a vocational course in domestic electrics, which he failed to complete. This was more down to his hormones than lack of ability. Within 6 weeks of meeting, Judy was pregnant and shortly after that they married in the Church which is still local to them, St Mary's. Their first child they named Christopher after Judy's father, 3 years later in 1987 they had a girl, the very apple of John's eye, Francis (called Frany by friends and family), who is named after John's grandmother.

The Hooper family live in a former local authority house, a semi-detached in the small town of Sprockly. The property, like many similar houses was built immediately after the Second World War. John and Judy purchased it from the local authority under the 'right to buy' regulations. They maintained the house well, Judy loved to decorate and reorder the place much to John's annoyance and at times confusion, John did not like change much, just like he did not like gardening, they had gardens to the front and rear of their house both plain, easy to maintain but nothing that would win the Annual Sprockly Beautiful Garden Competition, John left that to some of his mates who prefer flora to football, which he thought plain weird.

John and Judy are happy, they have two great children, Christopher is just completing his Masters in Electronic and Electrical Engineering at UMIST with a job offer from British Aerospace in his back pocket. Francis having finished her 'A' levels last year with great success, was taking a year out before going to University to study English and eventually train to be a teacher. She was saving to go on a continental tour of about three months with her school friend Fiona prior to both of them going up to University.

They were rare, John and Judy, they did not have much when they started in their life together and throughout their marriage they had to struggle to maintain a good home and bring up two well-adjusted children. Over the previous 4 years both had lost their respective parents and through this tragic inevitability they became even closer in their relationship. John, while still young had plenty of opportunities to philander but valued his life's harmony, his wife and his children.

John had extended his garage to accommodate his prized mini but he was today working or 'playing' on the drive, to give him 'some good light'.

"Tea!" shouted Judy, it made John jump and he crashed his head into the underside of the bonnet of the car while he had been 'playing' with the engine. A few profanities later and he appeared in the kitchen, wiping his clean hands with a very dirty looking cloth, which he took everywhere. His hands were clean, the car's engine was spotless, he just liked to play the mechanic. Pulling back a kitchen chair he sat down to face the mug of milky tea Judy had just placed before him, with his usual Hobnobs. John reasoned the Hobnobs were the best dunking biscuits on the planet and said so every time he dunked one, "fantastic dunkers" he said, Judy just smiled and dunked her Rich Tea, which promptly fell apart when coming out of her own mug, John just laughed.

The kitchen had been recently seriously brought up to date. It needed it, until two years ago the kitchen was still basically a slightly modified 1950's kitchen. Now it was light, practical and Judy loved it. The kitchen window looked out onto the rear rather plain garden as did the mainly toughened glass rear door.

The ceiling was white and the walls were coloured pale green decorated with a clock, various pictures of the family and a large framed picture of the kitchen before any works took place. The floor was laminated timber from Ikea, the kitchen units were white with stainless steel handles from Ikea, the cooker, gas range, fridge, freezer, washer and dishwasher were similarly white from Ikea. The dark brown table on which the mugs were now resting on was also from Ikea as were the matching chairs. John did not like change, but did like Ikea, in fact most of the house was furnished with Ikea furniture. They had saved for nearly 3 years to have sufficient cash to refurbish the kitchen as they wanted it. They did not like debt, all they owed was a now rapidly diminishing mortgage.

"That smells fantastic" said John looking over to the range on which sat an Ikea white cast iron casserole with the occasional puff of escaping steam being sucked out by the extractor hood immediately above the range, which was from Ikea of course. "Liver, ox liver from Howes" said Judy with that look that said "why am I stating the obvious", she had been peeling potatoes while watching John from the window before making the tea; "liver and onions with mash how does that sound?" "Fantastic" said John who also knew the answer but still asked the question. "Don't forget the processed peas", said John in a commanding sort of way, "just getting the tin out of the pantry" said Judy adding "mi Lord" with a smile. John just loved processed peas with liver and onions, a real taste of childhood.

"Frany should be home from her job soon" said Judy, "I must have words with that girl about the state of her room", "I'm keeping out of that one" said John, "I think that would be very wise" said Judy, "since you put that TV on her wall, Frany has turned the place into tip, shared by most of her girlfriends from School so they can play games and watch films, that is not what bedrooms are for", "sorry I'll take the TV down" said John, "not on your life" said Judy, "there would be a near riot in the house if you did that".

"John" said Judy, "Frany is going out tonight to celebrate her pal, Joseph's birthday and will probably be late, and before you say anything she will be in before midnight, she always is, always has been, she knows the rules, how about us curling up in front of the TV and watching a few DVDs, I bought a six pack of Carling, already in the fridge, a bottle of fruity Hardy's wine and some snacks while at Tesco this morning, a nice night in, just you and me?" "What day is it Ju?" said John looking very bemused and a little awkward, "Thursday" said Judy, "and where do I go on Thursdays?", Judy looked instantly down, "the Pub!", said Judy a clearly annoyed response, "you know, I would love to just curl up with you, but I'm in the team, have been for years and you cannot let your team-mates down, we are at the Nag's tonight in a league match and we are riding high", "not in the least bit interested" said an apparently dejected Judy, taking the plate of Hobnobs off the table and tipping them into a white Ikea biscuit tin.

"Tea will be at about 5.30, so you have plenty of time to take that other love of your life off the drive, back into the garage and get yourself showered". Judy was inwardly smiling, she knew Thursdays were his darts night, and would not dream of stopping his fun but just wanted in a slightly mischievous way to let John know she existed, even on Thursday evenings.

John and Judy both turned their heads towards the downstairs hall, the front door opened, Frany flew into the hall, shouted "hi, off for a shower" and bounded upstairs. "Oh to be teenager again" said Judy, "what was she wearing? asked John, "have not got a clue", said Judy, "I am just concerned after seeing her in that skirt, well it was really a wide belt, more than a skirt, young girls should not be wearing such stuff", said John. "Hold on a minute you little prude, Frany is working and has to wear regular clothes and let us be clear you did not make any complaints when I was wearing mini-skirts at College" said Judy, "ah, but that was lust Ju, pure unadulterated lust and from that we created Christopher" said John. "Look John, modern kids know more about their bodies than we ever did, and if it puts your mind at rest her closest male friend, who is not her boyfriend, is more interested in his computer and Nottingham Forest than anything else, and I got that from his mother, who I bumped into at Tesco's this morning, nice woman with a strange choice in hats". "Does Frany know about condoms?" asked an air clutching John, "of course she does, more than you ever did at her age" Judy replied with a look of incredulity on her face. John was getting nowhere fast, so wiping his clean hands with his dirty cloth he got up from the table, drank the last of his tea and went back to clear up his drive and put his Mini back in the garage.

Judy, put the potatoes in a large white Ikea saucepan filled it with water from the tap, added some salt from an Ikea salt cellar put the lid on, and placed it on the range on medium heat. Everything looking and smelling ok, Judy went upstairs to see Frany.

Frany had been able to obtain a full-time job at the local Spar

Store, which was giving her for the first time in her life a little financial independence and she was loving it. Frany loved people, being naturally bubbly and gregarious and the Store obviously benefited by having such a bouncy and people friendly person behind the counter. Like Christopher, before her, any money she earned she gave a third to her Mum, who in turn kept it safe for when Frany needed it back.

Frany was not showering yet, but looking intently at the TV on the wall. She was wearing a green sweatshirt and jeans so Dad would be OK with that and her long blonde hair was tired back and her shoes had been kicked off. The TV had been connected to Frany's computer and she was lounging on her pink and purple duvet reading her emails. Frany's room had been originally pink in colour, however as she grew a little older, pink gave way to white and then magnolia and then all the walls ended up being covered by posters of long lost and for many forgotten revolutionaries, pop stars and pictures of earth from space, the room was a mess, the floor was covered with about a week's worth of underwear, blouses, dresses and jeans. "Mum, before you say a word, I'll get it tidy", "you said that yesterday" said Judy, "ah but I mean it today, Fiona and Joan are coming over tomorrow for a film night so I need to sort it", said Frany, "so let's get this right, you will tidy it for your friends, but not for me?" said June, "Mum I love you and you understand", "teas at 5.30" said June, as she left the tip with a smile on her face.

Before going downstairs she checked and looked into Christopher's room, it was almost a ritual, every time she went upstairs she check his room, not touched for four weeks but he has coming home for the weekend, so she went in and pulled back the covers to air the bedclothes, touched the curtains as mothers do, slightly moved a picture of a certain Austin Mini which sat on Christopher's chest of Ikea drawers, checked for dust, there was none, she smiled and closed the door as if somebody was asleep in the room.

Judy went down to check on her potatoes and liver. All was good, so she sat down on her kitchen chair and flicked through the local weekly rag, which comes out on Thursdays, with her now slightly cold mug of tea. Judy did not look her years, her complexion was near perfect, her hair was a mousey brown, she had retained her tan from the family holiday in Scotland and looked really healthy. She used to regularly exercise when they had their dog Sammy, a Jack Russell, who was sadly killed by a car few years ago, by going for long walks with him. She still walks, delivering her Avon catalogues and delivering products to her various customers in Sprockly, her commission paid for the holiday. Judy is five foot 6 inches in height and still fitted into a size 12 dress as she did when she first met John. Today she was wearing her usual faded jeans, a white blouse, covered in part by a well-worn brown cardigan, her mousey hair was long like Frany's and tied in a bun. On her feet she was wearing her much loved purple canvas shoes, now showing real signs of wear, she was content with life.

John came in through the kitchen door, "looking like it might pee soon, I chose the right time to fix the car", said John, "what did you fix?" said Judy in a sarcastic voice, "I thought the love of your life was in perfect condition", "well Ju, it was not exactly a fix, or a repair or indeed maintenance, but more like a bit of polishing and cleaning", said a distracted John as he proceeded to wash his clean hands like a surgeon does at the kitchen sink, the mucky rag still hanging out of the pocket of his overalls, which were also rather clean. "Give me a kiss, my little mucky mechanic" said Judy as she leaned over to kiss John as he carefully washed his clean hands. They exchanged a kiss leaving a smile on both faces and Judy got down to setting the table for tea.

"Chris should be back in time for a pint on Friday night, looking forward to it already", said John as he left the kitchen to go upstairs, "nothing new there then" said Judy with a wide smile on her face, she loved the relationship John had with his children, loved them all. "Hold it, even if Chris does not make it in time, you're going out to have a stag party for a sixty-five-year-old who is getting married on Saturday" said Judy with a giggle, "and your cavorting with the ladies of the Mothers' Union at a hen party" came a laughing reply from John upstairs.

Frany was already in the shower, so John went into his bedroom and relaxed on his bed, minus the clean overalls he had been wearing, now just wearing his boxers and 'T' shirt carrying a faded picture of the Loch Ness Monster, a souvenir from a Scottish holiday years ago.

Being an early post war house the property had one bathroom, upstairs, comprising toilet, sink and a shower cubicle, the bath had been removed about 10 years ago when John had remodelled the room, as is downstairs most of the fittings were from Ikea, except the shower which he bought from B&Q in the sale. There was a downstairs loo just off the front door and in the hall. The house, by design was nothing really special, but the home was.

Frany was down first for tea, hair wrapped in a brown towel, body wrapped in blue bath towel, all wrapped up in a red bath robe with a hood and a United badge, the very picture of colour incoordination. By now the gorgeous aroma of liver and onions simmering slowly in Judy's house famous gravy was pervading the whole of the downstairs. As usual without saying a word Frany took her usual seat at the table and texted and texted and texted away, as if on another planet.

"Where's my United robe?" came the shout from John upstairs, no response was offered by either Judy or Frany. Judy just kept on preparing the mash and Frany just kept on texting. Moments later John came down still with wet hair wrapped in a bath towel and wearing Judy's rather tight Ikea white bathrobe, Frany didn't look up, she just continued to text. Judy gave John a knowing smile and he sat down awaiting his much wanted tea with his wet hair splashing the table.

"Dad, I know I have asked before, but when can we have a TV

in the kitchen, meal times are so boring?" asked Frany, who still appeared to be texting while talking. "Sorry, it is not going to happen, we have TVs in the front room, all the bedrooms can we not have a room without a set and try, at least in one room to have a conversation?" said a still wet John, the still texting Frany than asked "what do you want to talk about? "how about life before text?", replied a frustrated John and June just smiled as she finished off preparing the mash.

The meal served and June sat down at last to enjoy her tea. Frany reluctantly put down her phone and spoke, "off out tonight for Joseph's birthday party, can you pick me up Dad, it could be quite late so want a safe journey home?', June butted in "I'll do it love, your Dad's playing with his pals, throwing darts as usual", "sorry forgot it was Thursday" said Frany, "where you playing tonight?", "an away match at the Nags ", John's reply was not instant as he was fighting with a piece of rather hot meat. "How on earth is that an away match, the Nags is only a quarter of mile away from The Plough?", "ah but it is not The Plough, so it is classed away", said John still delaying replies while dealing with his hot tea. Getting up a dripping John asked, "Anyone want a drink while I let me tea cool a bit?". "Water is fine" said June, "me too" said Frany. John drew three Ikea glasses from the cupboard and promptly filled them from his Ikea tap with cold water.

A loud clap of thunder virtually shook the house, "ruddy hell, that was loud", a surprised and little shaken John said, "said it would rain, so where is your party Frany?", "the back room of The Plough", "that's a pub", said John in a rather louder voice than normal, "yes Dad The Plough is a pub", "don't be funny with me young lady" responded John, "Joseph is 18, most of his friends are 18, as I am if you remember so it is legal" said a rather bemused Frany, "not happy, any adults going?" said a now grumpy dad, "we are now adults dad, it happens when you become 18, you didn't make this much fuss when Chris had his party in the same back room for his 18th, but to put your mind at rest Joseph's mum is coming along, as Joseph's Dad is part of The Nag Head's team so you will meet him later". "Good, great, at last, a sensible party", said John tucking into his tea, "this is gorgeous, as always love", John spoke through a full mouth, June just smiled her smile and Frany ate hers with the same enthusiasm.

Another clap of thunder and outside they all could see the sky open and torrential rain fall and a darkness descend.

"Going to watch the 6 o'clock news" said John, his plate having been cleaned of gravy with a piece of bread so it looked virtually fresh from the cupboard, but he still looking wet and wearing a bathrobe far too small for his frame he went into the front room.

John was built with a frame that over the years had spread rather than grown taller, he stood 5 foot 11 inches and weighed in at 15 stone 5 pounds, a little over weight according to him, but in need of losing a good few pounds according to June. His hair was greying from an original colour of blonde and while it had been as long as the boys from Abba, was now more military, short back and sides. He did not smoke but enjoyed his occasional pint on Thursdays and at the weekends when June would join him at The Plough, where they sometimes, when they could afford it, had a pub steak meal for two. He had ambitions, like owning a new flat screen TV, his current tubed version was so out of date and he thought it an embarrassment, he wanted to take June for a great holiday to celebrate her 40th birthday and had been secretly saving up and was nearly there and he wanted to go a Derby match, United against City, his brother Stuart was a City fan and both wanted to go together however the cost is a problem as is for both of them, getting time off work, Stuart is a bobby in Bolton. John settled on the couch to watch his news and before the headlines had finished was fast asleep.

"John darling, it is nearly seven, you need to be moving if you intend to leave me and go to your darts match", June was gently shaking John, who woke with a jump, "what's up, oh sorry love, must have fallen off", said a still slightly wet John.

"You have a bit more time than usual, George has phoned and he will pick you and the rest of the team up, the weather is still pretty foul" said June as John slowly climbed the stairs. "That's George, good chap that, save getting wet; down in a bit", said John.

"Dad you are putting on the weight", Frany was viewing her Dad wearing his short sleeved darts' shirt which June had bought him a good 5 years ago and he loved it. "Your Dad's is trying to become the stereotypical dart player, all belly and beer", said June laughing, John just pulled the shirt out a bit hoping it would stretch, which it didn't.

There was a honk outside, George was waiting in his purple, rather tatty Ford Mondeo, the rain had eased off a little, so John slipped on his jacket, gave June a kiss, approached the door, turned around, shouted up to Frany, who had gone back to her bedroom to prepare for the party "Have good party my love, keep safe", "thanks Dad, see you when I get home" said Frany, turned towards the door to meet June right across it, he gave her a kiss, she gave him a kiss adding gently and quietly, "it is not often the house is ours for a few hours in the evening, hint, hint", "sorry Ju, George is waiting, cannot let the guys down" said a rather sheepish John. They shared another kiss and John opened the door, grabbed his rain jacket, tapped the jacket pocket to ensure his darts were there and left into the now heavier rain. John rushed to the car with all the windows misted up, tried the front passenger door, only to see Harry there, so tried the rear door to find Paul there, so getting wetter rushed around the rear of the car and jumped in while waving to June next to a wet Paul.

June turned from the door and closed it with her special smile, and thought, 'I'm still in love with that man, bloody darts!' and went off to tidy the kitchen and then look forward to a night watching her soaps.

5 THE VICARAGE

Tom was sitting in his study, listening to the rain, watching the gathering storm and loving it. He loved nature in all its varied performances and just marvelled. Tom had been the vicar of Sprockly Parish Church for 8 years and was feeling very content with the work he and his wife Georgina had done during that time. The Church congregation of St Mary's had tripled in that period of 8 years; sure it was from a low base but the figures as he saw them spoke for themselves by God's Grace.

Tom had been a soldier at 19, serving in the Yorkshire Regiment for 9 years and was proud to have served in the same regiment as his father had done. After his military service he put himself forward for ordination, always having that personal vocation and strength of faith. After going through the various and puzzling processes the Church of England put prospective ordinands through he was accepted at the age of 30 for training, he chose to go to Trinity College, Bristol. After two years he was ordained as a Deacon and sent to a parish in Aldershot for hands on training as a Curate.

This reawakened his love for the military life as well as his desire to serve his Church and his God. He applied to join the Royal Army Chaplaincy Department. They accepted him after he had served 2 years as a curate, he was commissioned into the British Army. His first posting was to Strensall Barracks just outside York where he met Georgina who was the senior Chaplain's daughter. Romance followed, the courtship was short and they were married in the Barrack's Chapel by the bride's father, eleven months later Georgina gave birth to the first of their three children, Zoe, 6lbs 9ozs, a year later Arthur, 7lbs 1oz. Tim followed Arthur two year later coming in at 7lbs 5ozs.

The day before he was due to leave the Army to take up Parish duties the IRA murdered 29 folk in Omagh, Norther Ireland. Tom was given permission to stay and support local clergy, give counselling to the emergency services and armed forces personnel as they cleared up the horror and also giving bereavement help to those who had lost loved ones in the horror. Tom often recalls that on that day and for the few days following he had never cried so much in total loving empathy with those who had died and those who had lost loved ones.
Through all this and other military conflicts he had been involved in as a non-combatant chaplain he never hated the enemy he prayed for them.

Tom and Georgina were so proud of their children and their achievements. Zoe was studying medicine at Bristol, Arthur was at Loughborough doing Sports' Sciences and Tim was doing his sixth form at Welbeck College aiming to join the army like is father and grandfather before him. The picture wall in the study was a mosaic of pictures showing the happy Wilsons across the years, most of the other walls were covered in bookshelves displaying a vast array of theological and natural history books, typical fare for such a man as Tom. He had a large old desk facing the window which over looked the 'vicarage garden' as he liked to call it.

The garden was well cared for, by Georgina, Tom just had no enthusiasm for gardening, even though he loved nature. His idea of enjoying the garden was having a barbeque with family, parishioners or friends, sipping his favourite wine and simply enjoying himself or sitting on the stump, an old tree stump, which sat in the middle of the garden and on which he would sit and think for hours.

On his desk was his computer screen, keyboard and mouse. The big computer thing was in the foot well with the printer to the right hand side of the desk sitting on an old Fortnum and Masons hamper box. He had two pictures on his desk, one of him and Georgina on their honeymoon in Rimini, and the other was a studio picture of the family in a casual pose which he just loved.

As the rain continued to pour down he completed the Sermon for the coming big day of George and Shelley tying the knot. He liked George and was hoping to be able to join them at the reception as both he and Georgina had been invited, but life is never simple as a Vicar so he had given an "all being well", reply to Shelley. Shelley and Georgina have been close friends for the last 4 years, both being members of the Mothers' Union and the Women's Institute.

The thunderclap startled Georgina, which made her spill Tom's tea as she entered his study. "Thanks Georgie", said Tom in his usual loving way. Tom was dressed in a blue track suit bottom and green sweat shirt top with the name "West" emblazoned on it, not exactly vicar like and Georgina was wearing her much loved and worn jeans together with a plum jumper which had seen better years.

She had put on a few stones in weight over the years of their marriage, Georgina was comfortable with it and her weight gain was mirrored by Tom's growing portly figure and she loved the occasional name when he called her 'pudding', which was better than 'Mrs Michelin' which he occasional used when she called Tom 'belly features'.

"Any plans for tonight?" asked Georgina, "absolutely nothing at the moment", replied Tom in a very up-beat tone, "however, I have no pressing Parish needs that I am aware of, the local darts derby is taking place at the Nags tonight and I have not been out for a pint for weeks", "go for it", said Georgina "as I was thinking of popping over to see Shelley to see how her plans and baking were progressing, I may be able to help", "touché", replied Tom, "go for it girl and if you could give me a lift to the Nags and pick me up afterwards it would be great as I could have more than one pint", Tom said with a longing look of thirst aided by his usual smile. "No problem", said Georgina, "I had better get changed if I am going to see Shelley and the regulars", said Georgina as she quickly departed the study. Tom looked at his sweat shirt, pulled it out a little, reading 'West' upside down and getting up shouted "me too" as he headed towards the door.

Georgina was already in the shower as Tom entered their bedroom. Tom went into the bathroom and stood in front of the mirror rubbing his day old stubble, should he shave or should he not shave, "I hope your shaving before you go out tonight", a voice came from the shower cubicle, the decision was made up for him Tom, he pulled off his sweat shirt, wet his face and applied shaving gel and proceeded to shave.

After shaving and washing Tom removed his beloved York City, replica shirt from his wardrobe and slipped it on. The great 'Y Fronts' as the shirt was known was, an enormous white 'Y' on a maroon shirt. Those were the days, remembering fondly his time at Strensall Barracks and his frequent visits to Bootham Crescent with his father-in-law, who just happened to be very friendly with the football club's chaplain, so complimentary tickets were the order of the day. Tom had been back to York on a sadly growingly infrequent basis, but held the club close to his sporting heart and wore the now very tight shirt with pride, also knowing that nobody else in Sprockly, let alone the county had one and it usually caused a laugh and a conversation which is what Tom relished in; people.

"You are not wearing that shirt tonight, are you?", said Georgina with more of a look of incongruity than a smile, "sure am", said Tom with a smile and determination is his voice. "Well I am pleased you are with people who know you and your extravagant and wacky dress sense", Georgina said with a smile and a shake of her head, "you must be bonkers" she said very quietly with a loving smile, "as she tied a towel around her wet hair and left the bed-room wearing Tom's oversized bath robe which she just loved, but the 'Star Wars' emblem on the back made it all rather comical thought Tom as he proceeded to change his track suit bottoms for his well-worn Wranglers.

Tom could smell his tea; it was coming out of the oven as he entered the rather large dining kitchen which came with the Vic-arage. Georgina was still in the robe, sleeves rolled up, with her hair wrapped in a towel holding a steaming casserole as Tom remarked "that smells absolutely gorgeous, my gorgeous", as he plonked himself down on his usual seat at the dining table, knife and fork in hand before the casserole had even hit the table. Tom sat there with his childish smile face on, and started to tap his knife and fork on the wooden table much to Georgina's delight, as they both loved to play silly games like that, it lightened the per-sonal load when Tom had to deal with serious issues within the Parish.

"Let's give thanks", said Tom continuing, "Heavenly Father we thank you for this day, for this food before us, for our love for each other and for our neighbours and friends. We also thank you for the rain that refreshes our fields and rivers. Bless our children, keep them safe, let them know your loving presence and be aware to them today and always. We ask this in Jesus' name. Amen", "Amen", said Georgina and with ladle in hand, chicken casserole was served to a Tom who was not now tapping the table with his cutlery. Georgina turned to the stove and brought over the vege-tables which she served from the saucepan with a slotted spoon.
Tom got up and went to one of the many cupboards in the vast kitchen and produced a bottle of un-opened red wine. "Now that is not fair", said Georgina, I cannot drink as I am driving you, and you have the nerve to have one", "yep", replied Tom, "not very often I get this privilege and for once I am taking it", "still not fair", said Georgina with a resigning smile.

"Do you want the radio on?", said Georgina, who had just sat down in front of her meal, "no its OK Georgie", I've heard the news, I just like to listen to the rain, your voice, see your face and watch the weather", said Tom, who thought he had a way with words.

"Great wine, this Aldi wine is", said Tom, "pleased you are enjoying it", said Georgina with a rather sarcastic tone, "lovely" said Tom, "and it so compliments this beautiful tea, thanks lass", "less of the lass", said Georgina, "that shirt is turning you back into a Yorkshireman again", "eh lass", said Tom with nearly a full mouth of chicken casserole and adding with some verbal difficulty "you can take the man out of Yorkshire, but you can't take the Yorkshire out of the man", Georgina replied smiling "well you can always tell a Yorkshireman, but you cannot tell him much", and Tom just laughed nearly losing his half chewed mouthful.

"What time are you wanting the car this evening Sir", said Georgina with her usual smile and using a rather forced posh voice, "well", replied Tom with an equally posh voice, "the tournament starts at eight, with pre-match drinks and canapes at seven thirty, and being the neutral spectator I will no doubt be asked to referee this encounter, can we say seven fifteen?", "your wish is obviously my command" responded Georgina as she offered Tom more of the casserole. "Oh, I do hope I do not get asked to score" said Tom, now in his usual voice, my arithmetic is shocking and somewhat embarrassing, I'll stick to seeing fair play is maintained and good clean humour is the order of the day or should I say evening", "guaranteed in that shirt" said Georgina with her usual smile "particularly the humour bit" she continued.

"I'll help with the dishes" said Tom, "no need" said Georgina, "these pots need to be put in the dishwasher, I'll do them, you relax and enjoy the rain".

Looking out Tom saw the clouds had thickened up a good deal and that it was nearly like night outside, the rain continued with the obvious threat of more thunder, he just loved it as he moved to the conservatory to get a better view and feel for natures' current mood. He sat in his recliner and watched the darkening sky.

"It is ten minutes passed seven", with these words from Georgina, Tom awoke with a startle, "oh my, must have been more tired than I thought" said Tom, "staying in then, nothing to do with half a bottle of wine?" said Georgina with her usual smile "oh no, I am not wearing this shirt for nothing", said Tom getting out of his chair and heading for the hall "and wine helps the digestion" said Tom as he left the conservatory.

"Georgina, don't think you have to come for me too early this evening, the matches should finish around ten and then there will be the usual post-match discussion and the Nags do fantastic food for the participants", Tom said this while smiling at Georgina and pointing to himself with his finger when uttering 'participants' and nearly falling over, not a good idea while putting your shoes on, thought Georgina with knowing smile. "Don't worry, your evening is safe, if I am early I'll come and join you for a shandy and a sandwich", "great" said Tom, "ready?", "remember it was I who woke you up, I'll be sorted in a moment'", said Georgina, "right see you in the car" said Tom as he picked up his Barbour from the coatrack and his flat cap from the peg behind the door.

Georgina, put on her water proof jacket with hood, opened the door to see Tom standing there, umbrella in hand with rain poring around him, "your carriage awaits my lady", Tom was trying to put on a Parker voice from Thunderbirds, but it was a shocking example of how not to do it, "thank you Parker", Georgina replied, in an equally hopeless attempt at Lady Penelope's accent. Tom escorted his Georgina to the drivers' door of their white Vauxhall Vectra, the door was already unlocked, Tom opened it, Georgina got in and Tom closed the door and rushed back to the Vicarage porch where he stuck the dripping umbrella into their outdoor stand. Pulling his cap down a little, he dashed to the front passenger's door and jumped in, very wet.

"This is some night Georgie" said Tom, tapping his now removed cap, so that the rain water fell onto the rubber foot-well mat. "All this, so you can wear your daft shirt", said Georgina as she started the engine, turned the car's lights on and put the wipers on maximum. "Makes a change from the dog collar", thought Tom.

The car pulled away on the shingle drive of the Vicarage and headed towards the Nag's Head with the rain still poring.

The drive to the Nag's Head was not a long one in distance, but in time, longer than normal as the rain could hardly be cleared by the wipers, even at full speed. "I see the street-light has not been fixed yet, it must be over a year now", said Georgina, "I am pleased this is not a busy road", she continued.

"I'm early" said Tom, "time to talk to Gary, the landlord, before the teams arrive" said Tom removing his seat belt as the car drew up outside the pub. "Hold it", said Georgina "I'll drop you under the coaching arch, you should stay dry that way", "thank you my Lady" in again, a very poor Parker voice, replied Tom, as Georgina manoeuvred the car under the arch and Tom jumped out, dived back in, gave Georgina a kiss and dived out again. Georgina drove into the pub's courtyard, did an excellent three-point turn to drive pass Tom waving his hat in salute. Georgina gave a royal wave and gingerly went back onto the dark high street down to Shelley's house.

6 THE NAG'S HEAD

Gary the landlord had been up since five this morning cleaning his beer lines to be ready for a noon opening of the pub. His wife Christine had enjoyed a late rise but cooked Gary his favourite breakfast mid-morning, it had to be a full English and only when he was doing his lines, it set him up for the day, so he said and his stomach displayed.

The Nag's Head had been in Gary's family for four generations of the Forbes. It was a seventeen-century coaching inn and re-tained most of the original structure, although it had been ex-panded over the years. The pub had two bars, the lounge and the tap room. The tap room was simply decorated with open brick walls, timbered and plastered ceilings, the odd print depicting hunting scenes and the all-important dartboard complete with dedicated illumination and the requisite mat displaying the oche markers.

The pub had gained an excellent reputation for its food and had a dedicated restaurant, looked after by Christine which was housed in former stables, towards the rear of the pub but being served by a very well appointed lounge bar. They employed a chef for the restaurant and served food in the evening, throughout the week except for Mondays and Tuesdays. The coaching arch had been re-tained and across from the pub there were three bed and breakfast rooms. There were no guests for the rooms this evening or the previous night. Noni, their daughter helped behind the bar most nights as did their son Douglas (Doug) when he was available.

Gary had lit the fire in the tap room which gave the place a really welcoming feel with a gentle burning fire with logs piled adjacent to the fireplace, all looked great.

"What's for tea?", said Gary to Christine as she appeared carrying a case of bottles to put into the fridge. "Are you having me on?", she responded, "Cricket Club virtually cleared us out last night of every bottle of beer and cider we had, they were on a mission", "good night though" replied Gary, "good night it was", said Christine, "you knew little about it, I cashed up while you fell asleep upstairs or was it on the stairs, how you got up to do the lines, defeats me, just how many did you have last night?" Christine was keen on a response, but Gary hurried off to the cellar after seeing what additional bottle were required.

The pub remained in silence except for the occasional chink of bottles being placed on shelves or in refrigerators. Sheila, the daily help arrived at about 10.30 and started to mop the tap room floor, clean the tables and put the chairs back into some kind of pub order. After the tap room she proceeded to vacuum the carpet after similarly cleaning all the tables, laying out beer mats and correctly placing tables and chairs that had been moved last night by Cricket Club, who had their beginning of the season bash, in the lounge, followed by a formal, which turned out to be very informal meal in the restaurant, which for that night was for their sole use.

"Must have been some party last night", said Sheila appearing with all kinds of hats, streamers and other party gear, "you would have thought it was a kids party, rather than our Cricket Club, what a mess it was" continued Sheila, "all good now", said Christine, "all Nag's Head fashion now", said Sheila proudly. "We don't have any guests until Friday night Sheila, so if you could go over there and make sure all the rooms are OK, Gary did it on Tuesday, but you know how useless he is" said a smiling Christine, "will do Chris", said Sheila taking her newly found party gear to the bins at the back.

Thursday was darts night, and it was the Nag's Head's turn to host the event with a team coming over from the other pub is Sprockly, the Plough, a real 'derby' match. Monday, through to Thursday the pub opened at five in the afternoon until eleven and night, Friday to Sunday the pub opened at noon until midnight.

Christine did her daily walk around the pub, starting at the tap room bar, followed by the toilets, male and female, checking stock, till float, optics were well charged, and that glasses were all as they should be, then moving over to the other side of the bar which served the lounge to ensure all was similarly correct. From experience she knew that Gary was broadly useless in such matters, but he was an exceptional 'mine host'. Christine then checked all the furniture was as she liked it and that the restaurant area was ready for the evening business. Sheila was good, very good at what she did and Christine knew it but checking showed she cared as well about the pub putting on a good show, for it was their income after all.

Gary was draining off the cleaning solutions from his lines as Christine retired to the pub office to print off tonight's restaurant and bar menus. Christine did this after Gary had something of a Basil Fawlty moment and put our menus with over eleven spelling mistakes. Gary did not like that job anyway.

Gary's timing was immaculate, just as he was finishing the last pump and checking the drawn beer a knock on the pub's tap room door reminded him to open up, it was five o'clock.

"Bloody weather, bloody, bloody weather", in came a wet, yet smiling Brian, the usual regular at this time. "Usual", said Gary, as Brian was putting his wet coat and cap on the pegs by the door, "oh yes please", said Brian drying his face with a rather large and not too clean handkerchief.

"Its going to be a bloody wet night tonight", said Brian, stating the obvious, "did you hear that thunder, bloody loud it was, bloody loud" continued Brian, "sorry Brian never heard anything, must have been out of earshot", "out of earshot, you are going bloody deaf, it was bloody loud, bloody, bloody loud" exclaimed Brian getting a little excited.

Brian's beer arrived, a pint of I.P.A., good head, heavy body and stronger than most draught beers. As was the usual practice, Brian downed the first pint in one and as the empty glass was placed back on the bar Gary had placed a full one next to it, which Brian took to a table by the fire. Even though the furniture was correct, Brian as always to move a stool and chair so that he could sit as he has always sat.

"Bloody good pint Gary", said Brian as he gently savoured his second glass of the evening.

Gary did not tolerate bad language in the tap room or indeed anywhere in the pub and he had many an altercation with a foul-mouthed drunk as he or she were escorted off the premises, a clear sign in both bars made it clear that expletives would not be tolerated and that users would be asked to leave. "Bloody" was the worst language allowed and the rule was respected by all regulars, who seemed to use it as a permanent adjective.

"Any music?", said Brian, "there is nowt on telly, so I thought a bit of your nice music would be really lovely". "Coming up", said Gary as he went on his knees to turn on the pub's music system muttering "Doug keeps promising to move this bloody machine, my knees are not getting any younger". "There you go Brian, a bit of Barry Manilow", said Gary, "don't like Manilow" said Brian, "tough", said Gary smiling, as was Brian.

The tap room door opened with a crash, "have you seen the bloody rain out there, we must be getting a bloody month's worth in one night, bloody ridiculous", in walked Keith, his cap soaked, his umbrella ineffective and his coat dripping. Keith hung his wet clothing on the pegs by the door and placed his umbrella in the corner by the door, creating an instant pool of water. "Evening Keith", said Gary, "evening Gary", came Keith's reply, "usual?", asked Gary, "usual please", came Keith's reply.

Keith had recently retired from the local police force having spent his working life on the beat in the town and in the country around. He knew everyone and everyone knew him, he remained a constable all his working life having no ambition for promotion or greater responsibility, he loved the town and the town loved him.

Keith took his beer and sat at the table with Brian as he had done for years.

"Evening all", said Douglas as he came down the stairs that serviced the bar, "evening Doug", came the response from Brian and Keith, with Gary adding "how is your head from last night", "fine Dad, but perhaps now you know why I like cricket so much", they both laughed as Gary left the bar to practice his darts in advance of the night's match.

"Fancy a game Brian?" said Gary to Brian, "no thanks, I am no bloody good". Gary didn't ask Keith because he was no bloody good. Gary just played alone while another regular crashed the door.

"Great weather for bloody ducks", said a very, very wet Steven, a local hospital technician and member of the Nag's Head's darts team. "What is you poison?", asked Doug while Steven was hanging up his wet things on the pegs by the door. "You are getting a good puddle of water here" exclaimed Steven, "I'll get it cleared after pulling you pint, which one do you want". Steven varied his beers from night to night, "I'll tell you what I'll have a Guinness given the weather", "one Guinness coming up", said Doug as he started carefully to pour the black liquid into the prescribed glass.

"I'll have one of those as well, please Doug", a relatively dry Tom walked into the Tap room, Gary turned his head with a welcome "evening Vicar, night off?". "Here for the match" said Tom, "and a very good evening to all here".

"Rotten bloody weather", said Brian to the Vicar as he stood to approach the bar for another pint "certainly not nice", said Tom, "sorry Vicar, I must mind my language, sorry", said a head bowed Brian, "don't worry Brian, given different circumstances I may use the odd inappropriate word", said Tom now smiling at Keith and giving him a wink.

"Hi Keith, how is the planning going for this year's Sprockly Beautiful Garden Competition? asked Tom, "coming on, coming on well and I guess the favourite to win is our groom to be and member of the tonight's opponents, George, the effort he puts into his garden is amazing, do you still want to be a judge this year Vicar?", "yes please" said Tom "always enjoy the competition". Being a judge was also the main reason for the question he originally asked.

"How did you get here Vicar, your coat is hardly wet?" asked Gary, "my wife drove me and is kindly picking me up". "Here is your Guinness Vicar", said Doug placing it on a beer mat on a table close to the fire. "How Tom gets table service?" said Steven with a smile, "because he is bloody Vicar, oh sorry Vicar", said Brian, "thank you", said Tom giving Brian a knowing smile.

"I don't know where the Plough's team is, but some of ours have not arrived yet", said Gary, "probably the 'b' weather" said Tom with a smile. "You will be referee tonight, Vicar, we need somebody to be neutral on such an important occasion as this" asked Gary. Steven butted in "I thought referees had to be agreed by both team captains, according to the district rules", with a smile and a hand on Steven's thin shoulder Gary said "who is going to disagree with the Vicar?" "Just making a point" said Steven, going back sheepishly to his Guinness.

"Can anyone play?" asked Tom, "I have not played darts for years". Gary gave Tom a set of darts from behind the bar and they proceeded to play.

Diners were arriving for the restaurant and more folk were entertaining themselves in the tap room and lounge bar, the pub was going to be busy tonight.

7 OH TO BE A TEENAGER

Judy after closing the door, just gently fell back on it and while looking down her downstairs hall she was not seeing anything, her eyes and brain were not connecting, she was just happy, very happy with her life, not having many material things did not matter a fig to Judy, having a loving husband, two children to be proud of, a home that was not just a house, Judy had for her everything she wish for. She closed her eyes and opened them and saw her hallway again.

"Frany, can we have a talk please?" said June, looking upstairs, "I'm doing my nails, can it keep?" said a voice from within Frany's room, "please, now if at all possible", said June in a rather pleading voice, "Ok mum, just give me a minute" said a more accommodating and less aggressive Frany.

Judy sat at the kitchen table and poured herself a mug of tea from a pot she had just made as Frany walked in, still wearing Dad's bathrobe and her hair wrapped in the same towel. "Well Mum, I'm here, what do you want", said Frany in rather irritated tone. "Please sit, Frany, do you want a brew?", "No thanks" said Frany, probably cutting her nose off to spite her face, as she loved a brew.

"Frany, I know we have had discussion about things before and I was please how you responded", Judy then just raised her hand and asked "before I say any more I just want you to listen to me, I may not be the most knowledgeable or gifted person on this planet but I hope I have been a good mum and friend to you, so please just listen". Francis, then raised her hand and said "I'll have that brew before you start, if that's ok, with a biscuit?", "Ok" said Judy, recognising the atmosphere had become more calm.

With brew in Francis' hand and a plate of chocolate digestives between them, Judy started again. "Frany, I do know who will be there at the party tonight, I have not mentioned it to your Father as he would simply not let you go", Francis tried to speak, "Let me finish" said Judy in a rather stronger tone than previous, "Thomas Collins is not a wholesome young man, you know he has already got two girls in Sprockly pregnant and he thinks nothing of it, fortunately not all men are like him but he is predator of women and you should stay clear", "Frany let me finish, I also know he has been to see you at the Spar while you have been working, how do I know, I saw you both and what is more I saw him kiss you". Francis was blushing and now not looking at her mum, "are you going out with him", "oh mum you use such old fashioned sayings", said Francis trying desperately to lighten the conversation, "Mum, we are just friends, yes I know he has putting himself around, but he will not with me", "how on earth do you know that if you are in his company and having a drink" said Judy in louder voice.

"You have a brilliant future before you, do not, do not, through it all away on this philandering youth" said an almost pleading Judy, "Mum I won't, I promise", said Francis, "what has brought this on" added Francis, "surely not just a kiss in the Spar", "No this" said Judy as she banged a rather battered still sealed Durex pack on the kitchen table, "it was in your jeans pocket when I came to put them in the wash, you should be more careful", "I'm careful, that is why I carry them", said a now shocked but sniggering Francis. "If your father knew you would be grounded even though you think yourself too old to be" said a calmer June who continued "youth is to be enjoyed, it is beginning of your adult life and can be so easily spoilt for good for a few moments of frolicking", "why the old fashioned terms mum?" said Francis, "don't mock me Frany, I'm only thinking of you and what you can make of your life, I love you, your father worships the floor you walk upon, just think and watch what you drink, be careful, enjoy your party, go finish your nails and get yourself dressed", said Judy in loving motherly way.

Francis got up, went over to Judy who was still sitting put her arms around her mum's neck and kissed her cheek, "have no fears mum, I'm not going with that boy or any boy, I keep condoms in my jeans because most of the girls do, it is cool, and mum", Francis quietened her voice "I am still a virgin". Francis kissed her mum again and dashed out of the room, "don't forget your driving me tonight", said a disappearing Francis, "I have not forgotten", said a rather pleased if embarrassed mother.

Judy went into the front room, the TV was still on from when John was watching it and flopped onto the couch, then got up again, went into the kitchen and recovered her mug of tea and the plate with biscuits which had not been touched.

After a while Francis came down and found her mum watching her favourite soap, Francis was stunning, her hair long blond hair just shone in the light coming from the hallway, her navy blue blouse was tight to her slim waist, the newly purchased jeans fitted like a glove and her canvas shoes made up the outfit. The clothes did not in themselves make her stunning, her personality, smile, face, poise and manner stood out and were so obvious not only to her mum, but to all those who saw her. Judy set the box to record the programme and gave Francis a kiss as they both walked towards the front door picking up rain coats and car keys on the way.

The rain was still heavy so Francis put her coat over her hair, Judy did not bother she just dashed for the car. The Honda fired up first time and they drove towards The Plough. "Oh nearly forgot" said Francis, "I'm babysitting for Sam tomorrow night while she joins you at the hen party", "hardly a hen party; at the vicarage, get real, at the vicarage" said a smiling June, "and dad is at the old stag party at The Plough" continued Frany, "what busy social lives we lead" a still smiling Judy whispered into Francis' ear as she pulled up outside The Plough.

Both startled they looked behind them to see two ambulances and one police car speeding passed them with blues on, "by they are in hurry" said Frany about to leave the car "yes I guess somebody's Thursday night is spoilt" said Judy leaning forward towards Francis for a kiss. "See you later mum and thanks, thanks for everything" Francis left with a little wave while keeping her raincoat over her head while dashing for the pub's front door.

Judy saw Francis enter the pub and was about to set off when two more police cars rushed passed followed by a fire engine, the blue lights, the heavy rain made the whole thing appear to be so much more theatrical than real. Judy, indicated and did a U-turn in the road and headed home to see further emergency vehicles going the other way.

Judy entered the house somewhat wet just as the telephone was ringing, it was Chris. He seldom called home, he was like that but he just wanted to confirm that he would be home for tea and was looking forward to having a pint with his dad at the stag party.

A further spring in her step, Judy went into the front room, picked up her hardly drunk tea, went into the kitchen put the cold cup in the microwave and reheated the drink. A few moments later she was back in front of the television watching her recorded soap, hot mug in hand eating her biscuits.

8 FINDING YOURSELF

Sam picked up a now very much wide awake David, who had no immediate intention of returning to anything like a bed or in listening to his mother read him a story. He wanted to play with the toy car his father accidentally started playing music as he left.

Sam accepted the inevitable and putting the nursery gate up left David to his own devices and noise. David, however was a very bright child and knew full well how to open the supposedly child-proof nursey safety gate, but kept the secret to himself and his mother never knew how occasionally the odd biscuit would disappear from the barrel which was always conveniently sitting on the coffee table in the family room just off the kitchen.

The downstairs nursery was close to the kitchen so Sam could keep a close watch, so she thought, on what was happening while getting on with her chores, she had all the pots and pans to put in the dishwasher and to generally tidy the kitchen. All this she did with extra zeal and zest, after a while she sat on the kitchen stool, having taken a cup of coffee from the coffee maker, which was always brewing on the kitchen work top and cuddled the cup looking into space.

She reflected on the past affair with Paul and was happy that it had ended, she never loved him, he was just a means to an end. She could not understand how it started, however she was delighted it was finished and then tears started to flow, real tears of sorrow for what she had done and tears of happiness for a new start with Harry.

Sam needed to unburden her emotions and guilt and as she had done on previous occasions she phoned the Vicarage to make an appointment to speak to Tom. She pressed the pre-dial number for the Vicarage only to get the answer-machine "Thanks for calling the Sprockly Vicarage, the Vicar is not available at the moment, however if you want him to call you back please leave your contact details, thank you", went the message, Sam asked Tom to give her a call when convenient not thinking that he gone to the pub and that Georgian was baking with Shelley. There was an irrational expectation that a Vicar and his wife were somehow always available and certainly not at the pub or baking with a friend. Then she thought "it doesn't matter, I'm going to the vicarage tomorrow evening for a few drinks to celebrate with Shelley and other members of the MU her wedding on Saturday".

Sam had joined the MU after her last meeting with Tom and surprisingly found it enjoyable and now knew a good deal more women in the area and was building up her own social life. Sam had not gotten around to attending Church services yet, as most of the MU did, but there was no pressure and she had no real conviction of faith.

Frany Hooper was babysitting tomorrow evening and her ready meal was already in the fridge, Harry was going to The Plough to meet up with the same guys he was tonight playing with and against at darts to have a sort of stag party for a pensioner, Sam smiled at the very thought, but was looking forward to hearing the latest news and gossip tomorrow evening.

The leaving of the message had somehow quietened Sam's heart and she felt better with herself, while listening to David making an even bigger din in the nursery, after getting all his toys that could make a noise, make a noise.

Sam went into the family room and turned on the TV, turned down the volume so she could hear the nursery row and curled up on the couch intending to watch a few of her soaps that she had previously recorded.

Sam also got out her laptop to catch up with her social world on Facebook, she enjoyed multi-tasking, watching TV and watching and reviewing her social media.

After what she thought was a long time she awoke with a start, the nursery noise was still happening, the coffee cup was cold and the laptop was in sleep mode. Sam got up with a start and looked into the nursery, David was fast asleep, thump in mouth, little mechanical drummers drumming, police car sirens going off, a little red car repeatedly crashing into the nursery wall and a whole cacophony of noise coming from his rather large toy box. Sam looked in and every toy that could make a noise, was. The "little monster", she said under her breath while smiling. "Now to get him to his real bed" she thought. Sam carefully opened the gate, lifting David with both arms she brought him close and while cuddling the still thumb sucking boy she took him upstairs.

"I don't want to wake him", thought Sam, "he is sound, but he has not had his wash or cleaned his teeth and there is a chance he may wake up later as he has gone off so early". "Time to be selfish thought" Sam, "I'll run his bath". Sam, cuddling the still thumb sucking David, took him to his upstairs room and gently laid him on his bed. The coolness of the room and the lack of cuddles must have awoken David, who withdrawing his thumb let out a scream, for no particular reason but children of that age do, because they can.

"Bath time" said Sam, smiling at her now screaming son, "and no matter how much you scream is going to save you from the bath". David must have recognised defeat, as he just sat down on the carpet and stuck his thumb back into his mouth and looked at his mum.

The bathroom off the nursery had a high bath set about four feet off the floor, Harry's idea to save his and Sam's back when dealing with a baby and toddler at bath time. He designed it in such a way that it would be relatively easy to put in a bath at normal height or fit a shower cubicle, Harry was clever on practical things like that.

Sam ran the bath, but in the required bubble solution and obligatory bath time toys. Walking back into the nursery, David was still sat on the floor, thumb still in the mouth, "come on little man, time to get out of those clothes and get into the bath". Sam loved these times with David and he must have sensed it, for he struggled to his feet, without removing his thumb, but once standing raised his hands high so his mum could lift off his shirt. He then jumped on his bed lifting his legs in the air so his mum could pull off his trousers and underpants. "Good boy", said Sam, giving David a kiss on his cheek as she lifted him from his bed and carried him to the bath.

David loved his bath times and his toys, he just detested having his hair washed and let both Sam and Harry know when they attempted it. Sam wanted a peaceful night tonight so thought better of it and David just looked at the hair shower head noticing it was not being moved towards him and his mum had not opened the baby shampoo bottle, "no need for antics today", he thought, "I'll leave that for next time", thought David as Sam washed his face, chest, back, arms and let the water do the rest except the feet. Sam loved to wash each foot in turn while carefully holding a giggling David who loved his feet being played with.

9 MOTHER

Toni closed the front door which Paul had inadvertently left open as he dashed out. Tom went back to the door, with his usual look, "I need a wee" look. Jack knew that look and opened the door to let Tom out, he also knew that Tom did not like rain, so he would do his job and come back in as soon as possible and sure enough, Tom bounded through the door that Jack was holding open, skidded on the solid hall floor and shook himself to get rid of the rain. "Thanks Tom" said Toni, closing the front door and holding Jack's hand. "I'm not cleaning that up tonight", she thought "besides if this rain continues, no doubt Paul will introduce a good deal of wet to the floor".

Toni, still holding Jack's hand walked into the family room, sat on the couch, Jack curled up on her right and Tom bounded up and attempted to curl up on her left, but Toni said "down, down when you are dry", Tom being very obedient, just flopped in front of the couch resting his head on his front paws.

Reaching for the remote-control Toni, turned on the television to watch her favourite soap. When that came on, rather than watching it, she paused the programme and picked up the telephone and pushed fast dial.

"Hi Mum, it's Toni, ... yes I am still alive, sorry we have not spoken for a while, but I have some news". Toni tries to telephone her mother at least every other day and is always slightly irritated that her mum does not get the idea that she can also use the telephone, a little like, it only works one way.

Before Toni could report her news, her mother gave a summary of her current concerns, health issues and news of friends.

"Yes Mum, ... no Mum, ... really, ... I am surprised, ... no I didn't know that, ... you should see your doctor, ... yes Mum, ... oh that is sad, ... please give her my love, ... Paul can fix that for you, ...yes Paul will come for you on Saturday morning and you can dress here for the wedding, ... yes it's raining here as well, ... my dress is champagne as is my hat, ... yes mum, ... yes your room is ready for your stay on Saturday night".

"Mum, now my news, mum you are going to be a grandmother again", there was a silence and then mum said "when?", "in about a month", "what", said her mum in loud response, "why have you kept it so secret Toni, is that why you have not been to see me?", "no mum, I just wanted no fuss and Paul has also kept thing very quiet but I'll call Shelley after this call and tell her", "is Paul there?" her mum asked, "no mum, he's gone to his Darts Match", "what, he has gone playing silly games while you are month away from having a baby" said her mum clearly irritated. "If it is OK, I'll pack a bigger suitcase and stay for a while after the wedding just to help you with Jack and of course Paul", said more sympathetic mum, "OK mum, if you must, I'll see you on Saturday morning, bye love you", Toni hung up the call, "Nana's coming to stay Jack" said Toni, to her son who was now holding the remote control after finding children's BBC.

"Not over sure that Paul will be overjoyed with mum coming to stay", thought Toni, when Toni was carrying Jack her mum stayed for three months and virtually drove Paul crackers with her controlling ways.

Still holding the phone Toni, pushed speed dial and spoke to Shelley. "Hi mum it is Toni, are you sitting down", "No I am covered in flour, still baking for Saturday", said Shelley, "well I really think you should sit down", said a very smiling Toni, "Ok Toni now sat down on kitchen stool, what's up?", "Mum you are going to be a grandmother again", after a brief silence Shelley shouted down the phone "fantastic, congratulations, thought you were pregnant Toni, you have been glowing for months and putting on the tummy, Toni is going to be a mother again", "who is there mum?" asked Toni, "Georgina is here helping me do the baking and keeping me company while the men are doing what they do, when are you due Toni?", "in about a month's time" said Toni as she tried to grab the remote control from a reluctant Jack, "not much time then", said Shelley. "Speak again soon mum, if not before see you on Saturday", said Toni, still not winning the battle to recover the remote control from Jack, "Love you too", said Toni hanging up.

"Jack can I please have the remote control", a reluctant Jack handed the device to his mother, slipped off the couch, just missed Tom in doing so and went into the nursery. "Thirty minutes Jack and then it is time for a bath and bed" said Toni finding her paused programme again, "Oh, rubbish", said Jack playing with Lego, "any further comment and it will be now" responded Toni, there was silence from Jack.

Toni enjoyed her soap, picked up Jack and took him upstairs to the bathroom, fifteen minutes later he was tucked up in his bed with his favourite soft toys.

Toni emptied the dishwasher, putting all the pots away and rearranging some, as her mother was coming to stay and then flopped on the couch to watch further TV with the intention of staying there until Paul came home.

10 THE BAKE OFF

Shelley was just putting her first batch of scones in the oven when the telephone rang, hands covered in flour, she grabbed the telephone handset with some annoyance, "yes" said Shelley in her usual blunt telephone manner, that being totally different to her normal conversations, she just did not like telephones, "oh so good to hear from you James, Dad has just left for his darts match, he plays most Thursdays and even the coming wedding is not putting him off", "so you will be arriving, hold on a minute, I'm covered in flour and need a pen and paper or I'll forget everything you are trying to tell me", Shelley put the phone down and quickly cleaned her hands and grabbed a pen and paper from the kitchen table draw, "that's better James, now where were we?, you are all coming into Heathrow tomorrow at eight o'clock our time, fine I've got that, you are hiring a car and should be with us by one in the afternoon all being well", Shelley was writing all this down, including the 'all being well', such was the build-up of excitement within her. "James, I know these calls cost a lot of money so I will not keep you longer, just to say, your rooms here, will be available straight away for all of you so you can catch up with the jet lag and finally I am so looking forward to seeing you, your Anne and Zoe and Walter, words fail me trying to say how happy I am in marrying your father". Shelley did not realise it, but she was crying in her joy, "James, best you hang up now and save your money, love to all and see you tomorrow".

The phone was put down at the other end and Shelley, just stood there with the handset in her hand and still against her ear and just cried. Even though she had, had an excellent marriage previously, she was now experiencing a kind of joy she had not thought possible.

The doorbell went, "who can this be at this time?" thought Shelley as she put the phone down, dried her eyes with a floury cloth which gave her a ghostly appearance as she opened her front door to be met with a rather wet Georgina. "Georgina, so good to see you come in, excuse the mess and get out of those wet things". Georgina took off her waterproof jacket that proved not to be, but her clothes were damp rather than soaking. "Thanks Shelley, I just wanted to come over while the men were at the darts match to see if I could help in any way and also take a peek at the dress". "Well that is really lovely of you, can we start in the kitchen, I was, until James phoned, about to put the first batch of scones into the oven and prepare my other bakes", "pleased to help in anyway" said Georgina as she followed a ghostly looking Shelley into the kitchen.

"Have you been crying Shelley?" asked Georgina as she perched herself on one of the kitchen stools. "Didn't realise I had been until it was too late", replied Shelley as she looked at herself in the kitchen mirror and hastily applied a face flannel to the flour makeup. "I cannot think of a happier time in my whole long life as now, my emotions I guess are just getting the better of me", said Shelley as she tried to remove the last vestiges of self-raising flour from her face. "Tom has gone to watch or referee the darts match, so I thought I would come round and keep you company knowing that George would be at the match and perhaps help, but also and most importantly get a peek at the dress before the big day" said Georgina, now off the stool and putting on an apron, which Shelley has just passed her.

"Blow it", said Shelley, "I'll get cleaned up and take you to see the dress and then we can get all floured up later", "great idea" said a beaming Georgina. "George has not seen the dress, he does not know where I have stored it and to be frank, I don't think he actually cares about such things, love him, he just wants to get married to me, it is lovely". They climbed the stairs, Shelley in front and entered the small box room, which literally was a small box, small and filled with boxes, but having just adjacent to the door a small wardrobe with a single door that required a key to unlock it. Shelley removed a key from her bra, smiled at Georgina with a real girly grin and put the key in the lock and opened the door. There was nothing in the wardrobe but a hanging bag boldly displaying the name 'Jacques Vert' and a hat box bearing the same brand.

Shelley rechecked her hands were free of flour and being happy withdrew the clothing bag and carried it to one of the spare rooms just opposite the box room. The silence created by the anticipation from Georgina was tangible, Georgina knew how important such an item of clothing was to a bride and Shelley was almost in emotional shock over the whole forth coming event. Shelley laid the bag on the made-up bed and gently drew the zipper of the bag down. It revealed a most beautiful champagne coloured suit with delicate cream detail to the collar and cuffs together with a complementary silk blouse which perfectly matched the suits colour. "My word, you are going to look fantastic, Shelley, this is simply gorgeous", Shelley had not said a word, she simply zipped up the bag, picked it up and went to the box room to return it and pick up the hat box.

The hat box, she placed on the same bed and opened it with similar care as the unzipping of the clothes bag. Georgina was surprised to see the hat box contained three cloth parcels all branded 'Jacques Vert'. The parcel on top was carefully unwrapped by Shelley, who has still not said a word. It revealed a fascinator, in the same colour of the suit with a slight reference to the detailing on the jacket. This Shelley laid at the side of the box on top of the wrapping, the next parcel was withdrawn and unwrapped, to reveal the shoes, the same champagne colour and the cap of the shoes showed a real delicate reference to the detailing on the suit. Georgina was now in silence, just amazed at the detail and the beauty she was seeing. Shelley laid her shoes on their wrappings and then took out the third and final parcel, laid on the bed and slowly opened it to reveal her handbag, a beautiful leather creation, in the same champagne colour, matt in finish with gold fittings but no detailing. "I wanted the handbag reasonably plain", said Shelley finally speaking "my gold jewellery will complement the bags fittings, "well, as they say up North, Shelley, 'I'm gob smacked', your outfit is beautiful" said a rather surprised and a little jealous Georgina, who was planning to wear the same outfit she had worn at her niece's baptism 3 years ago. "It cost me a bomb, I dare not tell George how much I spent on it, but I want the day to be special even though he thinks the whole process is slightly balmy and a waste of money, said Shelley as she carefully wrapped up her precious items in their cloth parcels and replaced them in the hat box. "Shelley you dressed in that, will make it more than special", said Georgina still catching her breath at what she had seen and been really bowled over by.

"While George is having a small stag party at The Plough tomorrow night, please come over to the vicarage for a little get together with the crowd from the MU, most are coming and it may help to quieten your nerves", "that sounds really good Georgie, thanks I will, I don't see why the men should have all the fun" said Shelley laughing, "I think the real laugh will be seeing George in a formal suit without a cap", they both laughed as they proceeded to return the hat box to its wardrobe, Shelley locked the door and put the key back into her bra. "Nearly lost the key in the bath earlier today" said Shelley, now blushing and remembering the circumstances, "how was that" a quizzical Georgina asked, "don't ask", said Shelley, "let's just say it got a little wet" said a very blushing Shelley.

Back in the kitchen they both put on their aprons, Shelley turned on the radio, tuned to their local station, and while they mixed, measured and baked they sang along with the songs and wiggled as women over 40 do when doing things to music. They heard a traffic report that there was a major hold up on the outskirts of Sprockly following an incident, but both thought nothing more of it, they were happy. The telephone in the hall rang, Shelley, wiped her hands took her apron off and left the kitchen.

After a few minutes Georgina heard Shelley shout, "Toni is going to be a mother again", Georgina smiled and recalled that having recently seen Toni at the local Spar, she thought there was bump under her coat.

Shelley came back into the kitchen with an even broader smile on her face than before. She put on her apron and said "I feel like celebrating now, but cakes are never good when the baker is drunk" they both laughed and got on with their floury creations, wiggling as they did and talked about babies.

Time passed, they were enjoying each other's company and being thoroughly happy with their evenings' endeavours, they had been having fun while preparing just part of the wedding feast.

11 THE ONE WAY JOURNEY

"This weather is shocking", said George, staring straight ahead while his wipers worked as fast as they could and the sound of his demister blowing almost drowning out his voice. "I don't know if it is the car that stinks or our four wet bodies", said a laughing Harry, "probably the car", said George, "sorry, I'm planning to get the thing cleaned up tomorrow morning before the family arrive and my mower petrol can in the boot is not helping, just in case you can smell a little petrol, but yes it is a bit smelly, but the weather does not help" said George still staring diligently ahead with his cap firmly placed on his head.

"Who's coming in your family George?", said a Harry not really bothered, but it made a pleasant start to the conversation, "oh I am so pleased, my son James, wife Ann and grandkids, Zoe and Walter", said a still staring George replying, "quite a collection", said John, wiping his sleeve against the misted up window of the car, "I am so looking forward to seeing them, they fly into Heathrow tomorrow" said a George who has not changed his viewing stance of staring straight ahead through his racing wipers. "Where are they coming from?" said Harry with a surprising tone of interest, "Canada, he is a structural engineer and doing very well for himself out there" said a George still staring ahead.

"Hasn't this car got air-con?", asked a frustrated Harry, who was trying to look out of his side window. "Yes, it has", said George, with a touch of indignation, "it just needs re-gassing" he added.

"How is your garden John", asked a mischievous George as he stared through the misty windscreen, with wipers and blowers going as fast as they could, "the gardens fine, thanks George, just don't like doing it" said John wiping his misty side window, "get a gardener" said Harry, "would if I had your money", retorted John, "but I don't, anyway prefer my cars" said John while still wiping his window, "it is only a pity George does not put as much effort into his car as he does his garden", laughed Harry, "you leave my car out of this Harry", said George still trying to see through the windscreen.

"Sorry George did not mean to upset you, you have been very kind in offering to drive on this filthy night, at least three of us can have a drink", said Harry, "cheers" said Paul, "I love the Gold Top the Nag's sells, pure nectar" said Paul smiling at John.

"Got your arrows George?", said a smiling Harry, "OK, I checked before I left tonight", "imagine going to a darts' match and having no darts", sniggered Harry, "a sign of nerves building up for the big day?" said John staring out of a heavily misted window. "My next car will have air-con that is fully gassed" said George raising his voice and changing the subject.

"We lost on our last visit to the Nag's" said John, "yes, and not one of us won our games, it was a total bloody whitewash", said Harry tapping his darts in his breast pocket, "but tonight", he continued "we are going to destroy them, we are not going back with the wooden spoon again", "hey the wooden spoon who has it?" said John jumping into the conversation, "it must be back at the Plough", said George still staring ahead, "I'm sure I saw it hung behind the tap room bar" said Paul, "I hope not having it is not an omen", said a smiling Harry.

"Guys, guys, guys, I know this is not the ideal moment or loca-tion", said Paul with a beaming face, "but I am proud and pleased to announce that I am going to be a father again", "that makes me a grandfather" said George, still steering with his nose nearly on the windscreen, "fantastic" added George, "when is baby due?" asked John, "in about a month's time", said Paul, "you kept that secret well hidden Paul you old dog", said a smiling John. "Another party" said Harry.

The car came to a halt at the only set of traffic lights in Sprockly, the rain was still pouring down to such an extent that the road drains had failed and the road surface resembled a river.

"Nearly there" said George, why he said that mystified his passengers, given that they had all lived in Sprockly for years and they shook their heads and smiled. George moved off after getting the green light. The car climbed up the hill towards the Nag's Head into darkness save for the lights on George's purple delight. "These bloody street lights have been down for weeks", said a George still staring ahead through his racing wipers.

The Nag's Head was on the right and through the rain George could just make out the drive into the pub's courtyard, he indicated right, the car's engine stuttered slightly as George made his right turn and then it stalled. "Come on George get this wreck moving, I'm more than thirsty", said a John, still wiping his sleeve to clear his window.

George tried to restart the engine just as a fully loaded quarry truck came over the brow of the hill at speed heading towards Sprockly.

With the lack of lighting, pouring rain and being out of immediate sight, the lorry hit the now stationary car fully on its left side and spun it back to the other side of the road to be hit by supermarket articulated truck coming up the hill.

The sound of the rain ceased, indeed the sound of the truck engines could not be heard, there was a silence that perhaps lasted less than a second. The car burst into flames, not suddenly, but a flash appeared at the rear of the now well crushed vehicle and then spread quickly to engulf the car's interior, blowing out the rear and front windscreens. The fire ball lit up the street with varying colours of yellow and orange it roared for a few seconds and then the flames declined simply engulfing the car and its occupants

In the very wet low light, both shaken truck drivers got out of the respective cabs from the safer side of their vehicles and ran towards the now blazing car, there was no sign of movement within the vehicle only flames and still human forms. The driver from the quarry truck grasped at the front door handle, but the door would not move, neither would any of the other doors. The side windows were amazingly in place but the front screen was totally grazed and resting on the bonnet. The rear window was just blackened by the flame and hanging open held to the car by burning rubber seals. The quarry driver dashed back to his truck to come back with a hammer and smashed the front offside window only for the flames to shoot out of the now broken window and scorch the driver's face and hands.

The supermarket driver, dashed up to the pub, which was now well illuminated by the flames coming from the blazing car.

12 WHAT THE …

"Was that thunder?" said a slightly surprised Gary, as he pulled his darts from the board, "bloody hell" said Brian in a shout, we have a fire out there. Brian dropped the curtain and dashed to the door just as the supermarket driver ran through the door.

"Phone 999", the driver shouted, dripping wet, with the look of shear horror on his face, "we have a major accident out here and I don't think anyone has survived in the car", said a very shocked, wet and shaking driver.

Most rushed outside to see if they could help while Doug called 999.

The emergency telephone call was picked up almost immediately, "There has been a major accident outside the Nag's Head, Sprockly, all I know is that a car has been involved and it is on fire, yes we will need all the emergency services, please hurry….my name Douglas Forbes, please hurry, please hurry". Doug dropped the phone and went outside.

The flames in the car had died down a little and despite the rain which had not eased off, there was a sweet smell in the air of burned meat, petrol and pungent smouldering rubber.

Traffic had now built up on both sides of the accident and the lorry drivers were doing a great job of holding the traffic back and suggesting U-turns were in order.

Keith shouted to Doug "have you called the Police?", "yes I have", shouted Doug, replying in a curt manner, brought on by the shock of it all, like all there who had not seen anything like this before.

Keith pulled his mobile phone from his pocket and called the Police Station. "Desk Sergeant please, no I will not hold, put me through immediately, this is former PC Keith Simson and this is an emergency", after a few seconds, "Hi Keith, what's up", said a rather dozy but calm Desk Sergeant, "Is that you Simon?", said a very wet and agitated Keith, "Sure is, what is the emergency", "there has been a major accident outside the Nag's Head in Sprockly, we have fatalities, a still burning car and traffic is backing up both ways making it almost impossible for the emergency services to get through". "I saw there had been an incident report, I'll up the priority straight away, keep your mobile on" said Sgt Simon Gregg. Keith, put his phone in his trouser pocket and went back to try and keep folk away from the now very hot and steaming car.

Tom had seen similar destruction and death in his time in Northern Ireland but he never, in his worst nightmares had he expected to see such a seen in Sprockly. He asked the locals from the pub, who were now very wet and shocked to encourage the vehicles who were blocking the road to turnaround so that emergency vehicles could get through. In their collective daze, they all did as Tom asked of them and they gave further assistance to the Lorry drivers.

Tom tried to open one of the doors, but just succeeded in burning his hand, Keith had a similarly burnt hand, but both realised there was absolutely nothing that could done of any value.

Doug went back to the pub, drew back all the curtains, turned all the lights on in the vain hope of offering more illumination to the tragedy.

The lorries lights were still on and they offered some help and the rain just kept on falling.

Vehicles were gradually turning around to find alternative routes and then the first sign of a blue light, it was difficult to make out what it was, and then another blue light and then another, and another.

The first vehicle that arrived was a paramedic ambulance, the two crew members rushed over to the now smoking car and just froze in the horror that they saw. Using their torches, they could make out four adult bodies, three had their faces burned to the bone the other's face was hidden by a still smouldering cap with his right hand grasping the steering wheel.

"Sadly we can't do anything until the Fire Service have made the vehicle safe", said a now very wet and shaken paramedic as he spoke to Tom and Keith, "However I am certain there are no survivors, this is the worst incident I have seen in my 10 plus years of attending incidents", said the paramedic as he and his colleague went back to their vehicle to radio in their findings. One paramedic, before getting into his ambulance bent over a road drain to be sick.
Tom went over to the ambulance and pointed out to the paramedic, now wiping his mouth, that perhaps the lorry drivers may need some attention given the shock they had just been through. The paramedic grabbed a bag and went in the direction Tom pointed leaving his colleague to continue with his radio report.

The fire engine arrived at the same as the first police car. The spot lights on the fire engine were turned on as the fire crew undertook their well drilled work in checking the vehicle, after being given the nod by the paramedics they proceeded to cut the roof of the car off with such speed it surprised the on lookers, who were many by now. The doors were pulled off and immediately the paramedics examined the bodies, as expected there was no life signs, just dead men, who were going to a darts match.

"Didn't expect to see you here Vicar", said a police inspector, who was now taking charge of the incident. "Came to watch the match, the darts match at the Nags", said a shocked and wet Tom. "However, Inspector, I know who the occupants of the car are, they are all local men, members of The Plough's dart's team and I have a feeling this is going to be a long night for both of us", said Tom.

"Vicar, please come to my car and I can take down the details of the poor chaps in the car", said the Inspector as he gently put his hand on Tom's shoulder.

Both men walked to the police car with its numerous flashing lights and got into the back seat. Looking through the front windscreen they could see the doctor arrive, who after speaking to the paramedics only made a cursory glance into the car before going back to his own car to make a report.

"Right Vicar, who are they and where do they live?" said the Inspector who had now brought out a small voice recorder as well as a note book and pencil"

With water trickling down his face Tom started to give his sad list "the driver I am certain is George Turnbull", "not the George Turnbull who is getting married on Saturday?", said a surprised Inspector, "the very same", said Tom, "the very same", "I know where George lives, lived", said a shocked Inspector, "the other occupants are Harry Easton", "from the big house?" asked the Inspector, "the very same" said Tom, "also in the car is Paul Howe", "the butcher?", said a now very sorrowful Inspector, "the very same" said Tom, "I know, I knew Paul very well we are, were in the same Rotary Club, this is a hell, sorry Vicar but you know what I mean", "I certainly do Inspector", said Tom, now very close to tears, "the final occupant is John Hooper", "that is the John Hooper who's brother is a bobby, I think in Bolton" said the Inspector, "the very same, the very same", said a now crying Tom. "I know all these folk, sorry I knew all these folk, not professionally you understand but through various contacts in the community, Sprockly will be shock", said the Inspector reaching for his radio.

The doctor came over to the police car and got into the front passenger seat. "Inspector, I understand from the paramedic, that you are the officer in charge of this incident", said a now very wet doctor, "I am", "how can I help you", "I am Doctor Shaw, I was asked to come by the paramedics, to confirm that all the occupants were dead, I have to sadly report that they are all dead, ambulance crews will arrive to remove the bodies very shortly if that is ok with you." "Thank you doctor, yes there is no need for the bodies to remain in the vehicle, they may be taken to the hospital morgue, goodnight doctor", "Goodnight to you too Inspector", said the doctor leaving the police car.

"Sadly the car has to stay in situ while my men do the pictures and measurements and the other nasty things that need doing after such an incident" said the Inspector, "I must see Gary at the pub, and see if we can use his back room as an incident room.

By the time Tom left the police car, a canopy had been erected over the wreck so at least no more rain was falling on the bodies.

Tom went back to the pub, which was now full of very wet regulars and previous bystanders who had come in out of the wet, some just sitting there, some crying, some hugging and some just drinking spirits that they only drank at Christmas. "Whisky?", asked Gary as he offered a glass to Tom, "no thanks Gary, I could do with one, but I think I will need my head to be totally together this night". "Where is the Inspector?" said Tom to Gary, "I have given them the back room, he is in there with some of his officers". Tom made his way to the back room.

"Not now Vicar", the Inspector sharply responded as Tom entered the now Incident Room, "sorry Inspector, but all the families are known to me and have links to my Church, at least let me help bring some comfort to the families". "Sorry Vicar, I did not mean to be tetchy" said the Inspector "we are all a little shocked by night's nightmare, I will be happy, indeed very happy if you could assist my liaison teams who will have to go out tonight and give the tragic news, but if you could kindly wait in the bar, while I get things going in here, it would be appreciated", said a now calmer Inspector "thank you Inspector", said Tom as he left looking at his badly burned hand for the first time. "We will need him tonight

Sergeant, that is for sure, maybe not just for the families", said the Inspector picking up his mobile.

"Gary, is there anywhere I can be alone, without having to use the toilet?" said Tom entering the bar, "come through the bar and go upstairs, first door on the left is our lounge, nobody is in there just make yourself at home". "Thanks Gary, I appreciate that", said a Tom as he lifted the bar flap and walked the stairs to the lounge, to have some quiet time with himself and his God.

"Given the seriousness of the incident the Chief Inspector has given authority for the road to be closed for at least 24 hours, so better get onto local radio and let the area know and arrange to post vehicles to block the road", the Inspector said to his busily writing Sergeant.

"Are you OK Keith?", said the inspector, Keith did not speak just nodded as he sat in the corner of the room, still in his sodden clothes with an untreated burnt hand and looking really nowhere. "Well done Keith, if you had not made that additional call to the station vital minutes could have been lost, it is just so very, very sad for our little town", said the Inspector while looking at various procedure papers that now needed completing.

The Inspector called over one of his officers and asked "are the two drivers of the lorries still with the paramedics and if so can you ask them to come to the incident room when they have been dealt with or find them and bring them here", the young officer, clearly in shock nodded his head and left the room, without putting on his raincoat, such was the force of the tragedy.

The two drivers were sat in their respective cabs when the police officer found them and he escorted them to the Incident Room. One had his hand heavy bandaged and part of his face heavily creamed having burned them on the car the other had his ribs strapped up and should have gone to hospital but wanted to assist as best he could.

A police mini-bus arrived at the pub with female officers who were led directly into the incident room and arrived just as the drivers were being brought in.

The drivers were asked to sit with a police officer while the Inspector briefed the female officers as to what had happened this evening and the procedures he wanted to be adopted in bringing the horrendous news to the next of kin.

The female officers started listening standing but were all seated by the time the Inspector had completed his briefing. The biggest shock to the Inspector was to find that none of the officers had received any victim support training and in reality what he had received was not really of much value now, he was to rely on their professionalism, humanity and strength.

The Inspector was most insistent that the four affected families be contacted personally at the same time, he wanted no third party rumours or false hope given, he insisted on empathy, calmness and eye contact and even suggested that if any of the female were not up to the task they could stand down without any comeback, they all agreed to proceed as directed.

"Where is the Vicar?", said the Inspector with his first smile of the night, "never thought I would ever be saying that" he said under his breath, one of his officers went looking and Tom came into the Incident Room within 5 minutes still with his hand unattended.

"First things first Vicar", said the Inspector as Tom entered, "ask the paramedics who I think are having a brew in the bar, to come and deal with the Vicar's and Keith's hands", the young police officer the Inspector had been looking at as he spoke, jumped up and went towards the bar, returning very soon afterwards with the two, now drying out, paramedics who attended to the burnt hands.

The Inspector briefly explained to Tom what was going to happen and asked as he knew the families if there was anything he should know.

"If I may, I would like to make the following suggestions", said Tom as his hand was being bandaged. "Shelley Howe has lost a future husband and a son this evening, my wife is with her now, helping her prepare things for the wedding that is not now going to happen, my wife has some experience in helping me in bereavement counselling, she is a friend of Shelley's and would greatly assist your female officers after they deliver the news" said a Tom with a now fully bandaged hand.

"I never put the two together Vicar, that is more than an ouch, how on earth do we handle that one?", said the Inspector looking at his female officers, "with love, empathy and care", said Tom. "So as not to overwhelm the situation with police, may I suggest you just send two and my wife can assist with the inevitable emotional response?" prompted Tom to the Inspector, "good idea, that is how it will be, thank you", said the Inspector making hasty notes on what was now a table covered with various pits of paper, in no apparent order.

"Toni Howe, is heavily pregnant and has a young boy Jack, I think he is four or five, Shelley Howe is her mother-in-law so in reality they cannot really be expected to give much support to each other given the news they about to receive, I would be grateful if Toni receives the tragic news with an officer with some medical training just in case the shock is too much for Toni and her still to be born baby", said Tom, now realising himself the enormity of what now needs to be done. As he finished speaking a female police officer raised her hand, "yes" said the Inspector, "sir before joining the force I was a registered nurse with experience of midwifery, I may be able to help here", said a slightly blushing police officer. "You are just the person who must go, you will be accompanied by two other officers to help with the young boy, thank you", said a now very pressured Inspector, making further notes.

Tom continued "Sam Easton, I know a little, she recently joined the Mothers' Union, I think too meet more folk as she is very much isolated in such a large house on the edge of town" Tom went on "she was very much junior to her husband and they have a young boy David who I think is three", "Oh nearly forgot, they have a beautiful dog, I used to often see the four of them out walking" added Tom. "I thought we were looking at 3 in the household" came back a slightly flustered Inspector". "Four are out walking, Harry, Sam, David and the fourth is the dog". "We will need two female officers and one male officer in attendance for Mrs Easton", said the Inspector curtly still writing on various bits of paper.

"Finally" said Tom, "we have Judy Hooper, she has a daughter at home Frany, who is going to University this Autumn, I would like to come with your officers to see Judy", Tom continued as he had an audience that were watching and listening to him, "in all my life, before I was a clergyman and since I have never come across a couple like John and Judy Hooper who are so obviously, totally in love with each other, they had a relationship that most couples could only dream of and now it is over", Tom repeated himself in a very slow and low tone as tears developed in his eyes and gently fell on his cheek "and now it is over". "Agreed", said the Inspector, "the Vicar and two female officers will attend Judy Hooper".

"Please get some refreshments, not alcoholic, we are on duty although I feel that perhaps we should all have a stiff drink after tonight's work is over", said the Inspector while making some final notes. "The landlord is making sandwiches and other snacks so get something eaten. I want you all to be at your assigned houses by 21.55 hours and to call me to confirm that you are. I shall remain here while the team sorts out the mess outside, so I will see you all when you get back, please come back here before returning to the station unless instructed by me otherwise, I will need a debrief as I have never had to undertake anything like this before, be professional, be police officers, show empathy and care, thank you", the Inspector turned from his officers as his eyes filled up with real grief.

"Chief Inspector Phelps please", said the Inspector speaking into his forces mobile phone, "Chief Inspector, Inspector Forbes here just giving you an update briefing on The Nag's Head incident, just confirming all four occupants of the car are deceased, we know who they are, they are all local and teams of officers will be attending the next of kin at the same time this evening, I have a great team and I know that by drawing such resources at this time of night it will put real pressure on the station and beyond", "don't worry about that Cliff", said the Chief Inspector continuing "how long will you need?", "very kindly the Pub has given the Force their back room as an incident room for as long as we need and given the scale of the even, I will be surprised if we can vacate before noon tomorrow", "that is kind" said the Chief Inspector "I'll send George over about three to relieve you along with an admin and investigation team so your guys can get some rest and well done Cliff", said the Chief Inspector "thank you Sir", said the Inspector, "Goodnight Cliff", the phone went dead.

The Inspector looked at the pub clock, not for the time, for no particular reason, just something to look at and stare at.

13 NOT A NIGHTMARE, A REALITY

The doorbell rang, "I'll ignore it", thought Sam, "I'm not expecting anybody and who would come calling in this weather and at this time?", the doorbell rang again and this time the caller was clearly holding the bell-push down. She picked David up and wrapped him in his bathrobe and carried her still dripping son downstairs to the front door.

Before she opened the door, she checked through her peephole to see who was there, an automatic porch light had come on and Harry for further security had installed CCTV, he loved his gadgets.

Looking through the peephole Sam could see three police officers, one male, two female and a police car on the drive.

Still holding David, Sam put the chain on the door and slowly opened it. "Yes, can I help you?", said a very cautious Sam. "Mrs Easton?" asked the first female police officer, "yes", replied Sam in a very worried tone, "Mrs Sam Easton?, said the same police officer, "Yes, yes", came back Sam in a more worried state. "I am PC Tod and these are my colleagues, PC Crown and this big chap is PC Hart, may we come in, we have some grave and very sad news to share with you" said the same police officer now showing her ID card through the small door opening.

Sam slightly closed the door to release the chain and then opened the door fully, the three police officers entered the hall of the house and Sam showed them where to hang their wet coats which they did in silence.

"Is this your son, Mrs Easton?", said the other female police officer, "certainly is, David the very love our lives, he is just three but very much aware and alert", said Sam now holding David very close and starting to be rather frightened. The first police officer continues, "Mrs Easton it would be better for all concerned, particularly David, if PC Crown could take David somewhere to get dressed and perhaps play for a while, just while we talk", Sam was looking everywhere and nowhere for answers to what was happening and she did not know what questions to even ask.

Without a word Sam put a still slightly wet David down on his feet, held his hand and put into the outstretched hand of PC Crown who asked David in a very quiet but clear voice, "where are your pyjamas and toys David?", to which David responded by looking at his mum, looked at PC Crown and led her to his nursery and the three stood still and silent until the door of the nursery was closed with a gentle click.

"Come into the kitchen, the coffee pot is on", said Sam, slightly shaking and leading the way. "Please don't say anything, until I have poured the coffee, my hands are shaking enough already", said a Sam now becoming really frightened and thinking it was news about her father who was in a nursing home on the south coast. "I'll pour the coffee", said PC Hart, making his way to the mug tree and picking up three mugs, the sugar and sweeteners were already on the kitchen table and Sam produced a milk carton from the fridge, sat down on her usual stool and just stared at the writing on the carton reading the name of the dairy, "the spoons are in the third draw on the left", said Sam now becoming strangely calmer, but still frightened.

PC Tod, spoke first, while consulting her notebook, "Mrs Easton, before we proceed, I just need to confirm that Mr Easton, left this house, this evening in Mr George Turnbull's car?", Sam turned, from looking directly at PC Tod, to looking at the ceiling and then looking back at the PC, "yes, that is right, he was going to his Thursday night darts' match", Sam paused mid-sentence and then continued, speaking more quickly and frightened "what has happened, what on earth has happened?".

"Mrs Easton there has been a terrible and tragic accident, Mr Turnbull's car was involved in a vehicle collision outside The Nag's Head Public House, all the occupants were killed". With that news Sam's eyes rolled, the full coffee mug fell to the floor and she fainted falling backwards off the stool, but being caught by a very alert PC Hart who was half expecting such an event.

"Well done Bob", said PC Tod speaking very softly, "if you can get a good hold, carry her to the couch in the lounge". "Oh I hate these duties Jan", said PC Tod with an equally soft voice as he lifted Sam up in his big arms and carried her to the lounge.

"While you try to bring Mrs Easton around I'll go and relieve Mary with young David, it would be more appropriate I think that Mrs Easton is comforted and cooled by two females", "Good thinking Bob", said PC Tod as she gently stroked Sam's head and slightly loosened the top buttons of her blouse.

"How is the little man Mary?" said PC Tod to a returning PC Crown still speaking very softly, "he is fast asleep, the poor boy, he is probably dreaming sweet dreams and his mother's will be living nightmares", said PC Crown is an equally soft voice.

PC Tod was seated on the couch at the head of Sam and PC Crown drew up a small foot rest and sat on that facing Sam and holding her right hand and gently stroking it. "Do you think we should call an ambulance Jan?", said PC Crown never having experienced this situation before, "no, not yet Mary, we will know more when she comes around".

"The young boy is fast asleep, I have lifted him to his cot and tucked him in" said PC Hart, "I'll go and clear up the mess in the kitchen and go back to him", "well done Bob, you will make a great husband for somebody someday" said PC Tod smiling for the first time but still speaking very softly.

The two police officers remained with Sam for just over an hour before she started to wake up. Slowly opening her eyes and turning her head back and forth she saw the two police officers, "oh no, oh no, oh no, it is real isn't it, I have lost Harry?". "Mrs Easton we are so, so very sorry" said PC Tod. "Where is David?" said Sam very firmly now sitting fully up on the couch. "David is fine, Mrs Easton he is fast asleep and PC Hart is watching over him", said PC Tod.

"So is that it?" said Sam totally bewildered by it all, "Harry is not coming home tonight or any night, Harry simply is not coming home, this cannot be real, I don't have nightmares as bad as this" said Sam now pacing up and down in front of the couch. "No tears are a bad sign", thought PC Tod. Sam's face was white, where normally it is vibrant and colourful, her eyes were wide and a deep frown had formed on her forehead. Sam started running her hands through her hair "I don't know what to do, I simply do not know what to do, I am lost, I have lost my rock, my man, my future, my everything", said Sam, still running her hands back and forth through her hair.

"Is there anyone we can contact for you Mrs Easton, anyone who can be called upon to give you support at this time?", said PC Tod, "sorry, I cannot think, I cannot think, I am numb, mentally numb, never been here before and I don't like", said a Sam in a now calmer voice and tears were slowly forming in her eyes. "Please sit down, Mrs Easton", said PC Crown and immediately Sam sat down on the couch next to PC Tod and started to sob and PC Tod but her arms around her and she sobbed and sobbed.

"I'll contact the Incident Room", said PC Crown, "yes, you do that Mary", said PC Tod becoming herself very emotional about the circumstances.
"Inspector Forbes please, this is PC Crown speaking from the Easton's residence", "hi Mary", said the communications office in the Incident Room, "transferring you now", "evening Sir, this is

PC Crown we are at the Easton's house", "how is it going there, Mary?", said the Inspector pen in hand ready to make notes on a pile of notes "well Sir", said PC Crown catching her breath "the team entered the house to time, we met with Mrs Easton and managed to take her young son to play with his toys so that we could speak openly. On receiving the news Mrs Easton fainted and remained out of it for about an hour, she has now come around and is quietly crying. PC Tod is with her and PC Hart is watching the boy, we have asked Mrs Easton if there is anyone we should contact on her behalf and so far, she has not had the presence of mind to give an answer which to be fair is fully understandable", "thank you Mary, are you three OK to hang in there for good while longer?", asked the Inspector while writing his notes "sure are Sir, I'll come back to you when we have anything further to report", "thank you again Mary and please pass on my thanks to Jan and Bob, goodnight" the call ended.

When PC Crown returned to the lounge both Sam and PC Tod had fresh coffee and were not talking just staring into space. "Mrs Easton has told me", said PC Tod "that she has a father who sadly has dementia and is in a nursing home near Portsmouth, her mother who she has not been in contract with for a number of years lives in Kent, a Mrs Susan Kempt, I have the address, and that she has a brother, Thomas who she is close to, who is the Army, currently she thinks in Afghanistan but she does not know his regiment, I have made a note of his full name and date of birth in my notebook", said PC Tod reviewing what she had written. "There is also a cousin, Mrs Hilary Boundford who lives with her family only ten miles away who Mrs Easton is very close to and suggests that we make contact with them", this PC Tod said as she passed over her notebook with the cousin's contact details to PC Crown. "Please ask the Inspector to send a car and not simply phone, we can be so cold on such matters as this", said PC Tod, "will do Jan" said PC Crown as she left to make a call.

"Your name is Jan?", said Sam very quietly "yes that is my name Janice in full, but Jan normally, but on duty I'm stuck with PC

THURSDAY .... AND IT'S RAINING!

Tod", "my name is Sam, please call me Sam", "I certainly will Mrs Easton, oops sorry Sam", both smiled and Sam started to cry again.

"Resources are stretched the Inspector informed me, but he will do his very best to ensure that a car is sent to Mrs Boundford's house to seek assistance for Mrs Easton", said PC Crown as she returned to the lounge. "Where is the other police officer, that big man?" asked Sam, "he is sat next to David's cot, keeping him safe and probably playing with his Lego", said PC Tod trying make light of a very dark situation. "Ask him to come for a coffee", said Sam, "David will sleep now until morning, he is like a lovely lad, but he has lost his dad", said Sam now crying again and PC Tod held her close "thank you Jan", said a very quiet sobbing voice.

Sam started up her laptop and started to show the officers her family pictures which she kept on the machine, she spoke softly, crying had stopped now but her voice was regularly caught by a sob, however a smile appeared when pictures of Harry appeared on the screen particularly when David was with him.

After about thirty minutes PC Crown's phone rang, she got up from watching the pictures and went into the hall to receive the call. "Inspector Forbes here, is that you Mary?", "certainly is Sir", said PC Crown, "good now listen", said the Inspector, "Mrs Easton's cousin has been contacted and she and her daughter are coming over as I speak to be with Mrs Easton, I understand that their personal circumstances will allow them to stay with Mrs Easton for as long as she wishes them to stay", "thank you sir, you have no idea how much that pleases me and will certainly please Mrs Easton", said PC Crown. "Once Mrs Boundford and her daughter have arrived please check in here and then head for the Station your shifts are finished and you can report as normal tomorrow and brief me fully, is that understood?", "it certainly is Sir and thank you", said PC Crown, "goodnight Mary and thank you", the Inspector ended the call.

"Mrs Easton", said PC Crown returning to the lounge "that was the Inspector, your cousin Mrs Boundford and her daughter will be here shortly for you and can stay for as long as you wish them to", "thank you, that will help me and David. Charlotte, my cousin and I have been close since we were small children, she recently lost her husband Martin, in an industrial accident and strangely I was able to offer her some support never ever thinking that it would be reciprocated", said Sam still speaking with sobs. "Her daughter Annemarie is four so should be great company for David, but how a little boy comes to terms of losing his daddy I just don't know, I just don't know", Sam was still speaking with sobs but the tears had returned.

The door-bell rang and PC Hart went to the door, it was Charlotte Boundford and her daughter Annemarie, they came straight into the house looking for Sam.

Sam stood as Charlotte entered the lounge and as they approached each other with arms outstretched it was clear Sam was going to fall again and PC Hart caught her shoulder and helped her back to the couch. Charlotte sat next to Sam and they both cried and then in total sympathy without details of the incident so did Annemarie who tried to break up the cousin hug. They stopped hugging, smiled at Annemarie, dried their eyes and looked at the three police officers. Sam got up and hugged PC Tod and said "thank you Jan", she then hugged PC Crown and said "thank you" and finally she went and tried to hug the tall PC Hart and said softly "thank you".

Standing back from the officers and still shaky, Sam said slowly "thank you all, this cannot have been easy for you, but you have all been brilliant, thank you, thank you, thank you, I'll be alright now, well for the moment at least, I have Charlotte", Sam ended with a mouthed 'thank you" to PC Tod as the officers left to pick up their coats and hats. PC Tod returned to Sam putting her card in her hand "If you need me for any further assistance please do not hesitate to contact me, that is what I here for", said PC Tod, Sam leaned over and gave Jan a kiss on the cheek with a further "thank you".

The officers left the house and PC Crown contacted the Incident Room to let them know they were standing down and heading for home via the Station.

14 DANGEROUS DOG?

The doorbell rang, Tom barked and shot to the door, Toni had been dozing in front of the TV and initially thought it was Paul who may have forgotten his key until she saw the time, five minutes to ten, and realised that was much too early for him to return. As she approached the door, she said "sit" to an agitated dog, slipped the chain on the door, unlocked it and slowly opened it.

There in the dim light of the front door security lamp Toni saw three female police officers with a police car parked behind them on the drive.

"Mrs Howes?", said the lead police officer, "yes" said Toni, "what's happened, can I help?" Toni continued in a startled and frightened tone. "Mrs Howes it would be better if we could come in and a good deal dryer as well", said the same police officer, "oh sorry" said Toni "I was not thinking, please, please come in". Tom barked, "basket" said Toni in a raised voice and Tom, walked slowly off, ears down and tail hanging low, to find his basket in the kitchen. "Sorry about that", said Toni, "I am sorry but you have startled me and before I call my dog back can I see your ID", "Our mistake" said the same police officer, as they all withdrew their ID cards. "Thanks" said a very curious and frightened Toni, "you can hang your wet raincoats and hats in the closet, come into the lounge, for if it takes three officers, it must be more than a speeding ticket", said Toni as she led the three officers into the lounge.

"Please call me Sue" said the lead officer the other two introduced themselves as Carol and Audrey. "My name is Toni, now what is up, was I caught speeding last week?" asked a puzzled Toni, "no nothing like that" said Sue and she continued "can I just confirm that your husband is Mr Paul Howes and that he left this evening to go to The Nag's Head in Sprockly in George Turnbull's car?". Toni was rapidly losing colour and her hands were unconsciously rubbing together, "please, what has happened, Paul did go with George tonight to the Nag's, what has happened", said a now shaking Toni.

"Toni, there has been a terrible accident immediately outside The Nag's Head and George Turnbull's car has been hit by a heavy goods vehicle", said Sue never taking her eyes off Toni, however Toni interrupted her "is Paul OK, is he in hospital, how are the others? Toni spoke so rapidly and then the number of police officers being there, dawned on her, "Paul is seriously injured, isn't he?" said Toni holding her head in one hand and resting the other on her bump.

"I am so very sorry to inform you Toni, your husband, Mr Paul Howes, was killed in the accident as were all the other occupants", said Sue in a very soft and slow voice. Sue then pointed at Audrey to go make a pot of tea. Audrey went into the kitchen, Tom looked at her from his basket, quietly growled and watched her every move as she found the cups and tea.

Meanwhile Toni was now curled up on the couch with her knees up in front of her tummy and her head resting on top of her knees. She was crying softly, "why, why, why, why my Paul, oh my Paul, why?". Sue moved and sat next to Toni, she was finding the situation very hard as well and put her arm around her, which signalled Toni to start sobbing.

"How do you like your tea", said a very softly speaking Audrey as she entered the lounge with a try. Toni just raised her hand in a gesture of no and just sobbed. Tom had ignored previous instructions but sensing Toni's grief came into the room, ears down and put his paw on Toni's hand. Through her tear filled eyes she looked down at an obviously sorrowful dog and nearly smiled and patted his head gently.

"I want to see him, I want to see him, I want to see him, I want to see my Paul", said Toni in a voice that was getting louder and louder with a hint of aggression. In a softer tone Sue said "I don't believe that is just possible at the moment Toni, there was a tremendous fire when the car crashed and even I don't know how much that affected the occupants, it will be necessary to formally identify all the four victims of the crash but that will be in a while". "How bad was the fire, is that what killed them?", Toni was becoming nearly hysterical, "can I please have answers, can I please have my Paul, oh God this is hell", Toni said as she stood up, "I must phone my mum, she is all I have and poor Shelley, I guess she is being told her news, isn't she?" Toni raised her voice again "yes Shelley will be in pieces", said Toni in a quieter tone, "I want to phone my mum", said a sobbing Toni, staring directly at Sue, "can I please, please phone my mum?" said Toni picking up the phone and gesturing to the officers to leave her company.

The officer left for the kitchen, Toni sat down on the couch, Tom jumped up beside her and put his head on her bump. Toni speed dialled her mum, the phone rang for a good while before it was answered "Mum, yes I know it is late, no Mum I didn't know you had gone to bed early, please listen, Paul is dead", Toni was having real difficulty in getting her words out between the sobs, "there was an accident in Sprockly involving the car that Paul was in and all four are dead, oh mum this is more than terrible, I have entered a hell and don't know how to get out, George Turnbull was also in the car, oh mum I need you here now, please, please, please", Toni's voice got quieter and quieter waiting for a response from her mum, "thanks mum, I have three police officers here at the moment when you arrive I guess they can go, please hurry", said a Toni now more controlled than before. Her mum told her she was getting a taxi; it would be about an hour before she got to her.

Toni let out a loud scream and Toni held her tummy, Sue and the other police officers rushed in, "this is why you are here Audrey, please take charge" said a visibly shaken PC Watts. Audrey led Toni back to the couch and laid her down putting a cushion below her head, her waters had not broken but clearly something was happening and after checking she said quietly, "Sue better call an ambulance, this lady is poorly, her temperature is now higher than normal and given that she is so close to term and I cannot feel any movement from her baby, that may mean nothing but it could indicate that the sudden shock has caused some harm". Tom insisted on laying on the floor just below Toni who was now throwing her head from side to side with her eyes closed and displaying a strong frown on her forehead.

Sue went into the hall and called 999 asking for an emergency ambulance and explained the circumstances to the taker to ensure top priority.

Sue then contacted the Incident Room, "The Inspector please, PC Sue Watts here", she waited a short while and the Inspector came on the line "what is happening Sue?" said the Inspector, "we have had to call an ambulance for Mrs Howes, she is not only in great distress over the news but it may have caused some danger to her unborn, we don't know so we are taking precautions" said Sue "but I need your help Sir, there is a dog in the house, it is a lovely animal but it may cause some problems when the ambulance arrives and takes Mrs Howes to hospital, can you send somebody to ensure the dog is safe and we are?", Sue was doing a great job in understanding things thought the Inspector, "certainly will Sue, somebody will be there as quickly as possible, by the way do they have a child in the house?", said the Inspector looking at the notes he made from the Vicar's comments "gosh", said Sue with a surprise in her voice, "that has not come up, if there is a child I guess he or she are fast asleep upstairs, Toni, sorry Mrs Howes has phoned her mother and she is the way", said Sue now drifting back into the lounge and pointing Carol and mouthing "check-up stairs for a child, check-up stairs for a child". Carol got the drift and went upstairs while Sue continued her conversation with the Inspector. "Any feedback from any of the other affected homes sir", said a Sue genuinely concerned "nothing yet Sue you are the first, but please come back to me as things progress and well done", said an appreciative Inspector and not wishing to prolong the conversation on other victims, "this is some kind of hell sir, I never thought it would be as bad as this", said a Sue now sitting on the first step of the stairs, "hang in there Sue, you do not now know how much you bring to situations like this until the dust settles, you will see why this is such an important part of our role in the community, hang in there Sue and well done", the line went dead from Inspector, just as Carol came down stairs.

"There is a young boy about 5 or 6 fast asleep, he is well tucked in and gone to the world, the poor mite" said a clearly upset Carol, "just how do you tell such a young thing that he will not see his daddy again" said Carol as she put her hand on Sue's shoulder as she came to the bottom of the stairs, "don't go there Carol, I'm having a job keeping it all together" said Sue with very wet eyes.

Sue and Carol returned to the lounge where Toni was more stable and very close to sleep, "I am worried over the temperature" said Audrey, "I have slackened her clothing to give her some air, but it is not over hot in here, but she is cooking" said Audrey wiping Toni's head with a wet kitchen towel, all the while Tom just lays there looking at all present and occasionally growling.

Sue's service mobile rang which made Tom stand up, look around and then flop again, just below Toni who was now a sleep, but the sleep was accompanied by the occasion sob. "PC Watts", said Sue "PC Watts, this is PC Thomas, district dog patrol officer, I am outside with a van, I understand you have a dangerous dog in the house", Sue looked to the skies, "PC Thomas the dog is not at all dangerous, he is loving, attentive and very obedient, but", Sue left the lounge and walked into the hall and still speaking softly continued, "the dog's master was killed in an accident earlier today", "is that the one at the Nag's?", PC Thomas interrupted Sue mid flow, "yes it is" said Sue getting a little annoyed "your job, is to put the dog somewhere safe, no harm is to come to the animal, but he must be moved for the safety of all before his mistress is taken by ambulance to hospital, got it" said Sue in a rather sharp voice, "right got it, has the dog a collar and is it on?" said PC Thomas, "yes the dog has a collar and it is on, do you want to see what is written on the disc attached to the collar?", said Sue sarcastically. "I will ring the doorbell which usually brings all dogs to the door and if you can open the door I'll have a cage immediately in front of the door to put the dog in, done this many times, are you sure the dog is not dangerous?", said a now timid PC Thomas, "the dog has let three female police officers into the house, it has allowed us to go about the house, it has allowed us to tend to Mrs Howes the dog's mistress, does that sound dangerous to you?", said a rather agitated Sue, "look the ambulance will be here soon, please get on with it", said Sue in frustration.

The doorbell rang, Tom barked a little as he jumped up and ran to the front door, he sat by the door and waited for Sue to open it and he dashed out straight into PC Thomas's cage. He barked a good deal as PC Thomas put him in the back of his van. "The dog is a valued family pet, he is to be brought back tomorrow afternoon fit, fed and healthy", said Sue with an air of authority not knowing if she actually had any seniority over PC Thomas. "Fine, we'll look after the noisy animal, goodnight PC Watts" said PC Thomas as he climbed into his van, "goodnight" said Sue as she turned and closed the front door.

"Sir, this is PC Watts, the dog has been removed from the Howes' home, but the dog officer thought it was dangerous, may I ask you Sir to ensure that nothing happens to that dog, this family has had enough?", "Sorry, Sue, it was probably my description of a possible dangerous dog scenario to the Desk Sergeant when I called it in, the dog will be kept safe", said an Inspector hastily making a note about the dog, "ambulance is not here yet Sir, are there problems", "sure are Sue, ambulance service is well stretched at the moment, not only with accident at the Nag's but with the shocking weather there has been three major pileups on the motorway", said the Inspector passing his note on the dog to the communication officer.

"May I request Sir, that the duty doctor attends the Howes' residence as a matter of urgency to determine if Mrs Howes can be moved by police car to the hospital?", said a commanding and very frustrated Sue, "I'll get on to it", said the inspector finishing the call. "Collins please make sure the Dog Patrol know that nothing, absolutely nothing happens to the Howes' dog that they have just picked up", said a now rather flushed and out of depth Inspector, "will do Sir", said PC Collins, with that the Inspector contacted the hospital for their emergency doctor.

Toni was coming around was starting to speak PC Collins, "what happened?", said Toni, "not over sure, but I am really pleased you are back with us", said PC Collins, she went on "how do you feel Toni?", "not really sure" said Toni as she stroked her tummy. "Given the events of tonight and the shock to your system I would prefer to get you checked out at the hospital, are you fit for a journey in a police car?", said PC Collins holding Toni's hand, "If you'll drive it, I'll sit in it", said Toni, "Carol and Audrey will stay to look after Jack and then your Mum will arrive" said PC Collins.

"Let's get going" said a now standing Toni, more in shock than control, but nevertheless thinking of her unborn baby's welfare. "Audrey please tell the Inspector that I am taking Mrs Howes to the hospital with her permission and to cancel the call to the so called emergency doctor", PC Collins said with an edge of sarcasm as they gathered coats and went to the police car outside, the rain had eased a little.

On arrival at the hospital Toni was placed on a trolley and taken straight into the A&E unit and PC Collins having given full details to the nurses' desk returned to the Howes home awaiting the arrival of Toni's mother.

Toni's mother's taxi and the police car arrived at the Howes at the same time. The taxi driver was left to pull out of his boot an enormous suitcase which obviously weighed a good deal by the way he was struggling to get it to the front door. Toni's mother hardly looked at the police car as she approached the front door and pressed the door bell, before the door was opened PC Collins was at her side. "I am PC Collins from Sprockly police, two of my colleagues are inside the house", with that the door was opened and Toni's mother strode in without acknowledging anyone. The taxi driver delivered the suitcase to the front door and asked for his fare "twenty five pounds, sixty pence and a hernia please madam", Toni's mum spun around, opened her purse and gave the man thirty pounds and said "thanks for getting me here so quickly it is appreciated and keep the change".

She now acknowledged the three police officers, "where is my daughter, I want to see her?", PC Collins spoke first "I am PC Collins of the Sprockly Police Force", "yes, yes I have heard all that, where is my daughter?" said a rather irritated Toni's mother, "can I please have your name?" said PC Collins opening her notebook, "procedures and process", said a further irritated Toni's mother "here is my driving licence" as she rummaged in her handbag, "my name is Irene Jennifer Stiles, maiden name Godfrey and my home address is 5", "that is enough Mrs Stiles thank you", "now, where is my daughter?", "Your daughter Mrs Toni Howes is currently at the local hospital being checked over following the shocking news of the death of her husband, we thought it better to be safe given how close to term your daughter is" explained PC Collins, "thank you and where is Jack my grandson?", "he is fast asleep unaware of anything of tonight's horrors Mrs Stiles. "I need a drink" said Mrs Stiles, "it is OK, I know where the whisky is kept and it will only be the one".

Mrs Stiles returned to the gathered police officers in the hall clutching a whisky tumbler with as she said only a small amount of Scotch in the glass.

"What happens now?" said Mrs Stiles, "now that the property is secure and your grandson is safe we can depart, however one of us can stay if you wish until we have further news on Mrs Howes' welfare, oh and Tom, their dog will be returned around noon tomorrow", "I was wondering where the dog was" said Mrs Stiles.

"Sorry if I came over a little strong earlier, it is not every day you learn that your daughter is about to have a baby and you lose a son-in-law, sorry, I am not usually rude". "That is fine Mrs Stiles, do you want company until we hear from the hospital?", said PC Collins, pulling a very heavy suitcase into the hall, "yes please" said a very less demonstrative Mrs Stiles. "I'll be staying" said PC Knowles, "my first name is Audrey and as I have no family commitments it makes sense for me to help here", "thank you Audrey if that is how I call you, please call me Irene and let us hope the night beings no further bad news".

With that the other two police officers shook Mrs Stiles' hand, expressed their sadness over the situation and left the house. PC Collins phoned the Incident Room and informed them what was happening and they returned to the Police Station and then made their ways to their respective homes.

15 SALTS, SMELLING SALTS

Tom, the vicar, was being accompanied by PC Claire Switski & PC Francis Bloomingdale. Their car arrived at the Hooper's house exactly as the Inspector has asked. The rain was still heavy and the front door did not have much of a porch as the three stood there as Tom used the door knocker.

Judy was dozing on her couch while not really watching her favourite tv programme when the sound of the knocker stirred her. She was still a little sleepy as she stood up and wobbled a little as she gained her balance and direction.

"Who can this be at this time of night and in such weather", she could see and hear the rain was still coming down. She switched on the hall light and the outside light to the front door, adjusted her dressing gown and slowly opened the door.

"Oh, it's you Vicar, please come in" and then she saw the two police officers and stopped in her tracks, "what is it?, what is going on?", "Judy may we all come in please?" asked Tom in his usual gentle tone, "sorry, forgive me, just a little startled" said Judy, adjusting her dressing gown even more, "please come in, you can hang your wet clothes on the pegs by the door", Judy pointed to where the pegs where and Tom and the two officers obliged.

"Judy, I think it best if we go into your front room and you sit down", said Tom in a firm and yet gentle tone. Judy did as directed, sad down on her couch, turned the television off with the remote and looked at Tom with her big eyes looking for answers to questions that had not been asked.

The two officers sat either side of Judy of the couch while Tom stood under the now switched on room light. "Judy, there has been an accident, John went in George's car tonight to the Nag's, is that correct?" Judy did not say a word she just nodded her head and stared at Tom. "George's car has been involved in an accident outside the Nag's and it is my painful and tragic duty to inform you that all the occupants were killed in the incident". Before Tom had chance to finish his sentence Judy had fainted being caught by PC Switski who was sitting on her right.

Tom fell to his knees in front of the now still Judy and placed his hands gently on her head and said a quiet prayer.

"We can do little now until Mrs Hooper comes around" said PC Bloomingdale. "No there is something we can do and do quickly", said Tom with some urgency, "I forgot about this, Judy has a daughter living at home and she and most of the town's youth are at a birthday disco at the Plough this evening, can we get some-one to go and get her?" "Is that the Plough in the town Vicar?" asked PC Bloomingdale as she picked up her phone, "Yes it is, the daughter is called Francis and I think she is around 18 to 19 years of age, she will be needed and needed quickly"

"Inspector, this is PC Bloomingdale at the Hooper's house, we entered house at the time you asked, Mrs Hopper is out cold at the moment, having fainted when receiving the news, she is un-harmed being seated at the time, the Vicar is with her along with PC Switski", "Thank you for the report", said the Inspector, rum-maging among his papers to find the given names of his officers, after a short pause "thank you Francis, are you able to stay for a while?" said the very stressed out Inspector while making notes, "yes I can, however we need some assistance, Mrs Hooper has a daughter living at home, who the Vicar thinks is currently as the Plough in town at a disco, can an officer be sent to bring her home, we need her, well her mother will certainly need her?" "At the Plough you say, no problem, I'll get it done immediately" and the Inspector put the phone down, only to pick it up again, "PC Bloomingdale, how can I help", came the response, "Sorry Francis, what is the daughter's name?" said the inspector with a now aggressive voice, "same as mine, Francis" said PC Bloomingdale with a slight smile "silly sod" she thought.

"Mum, what did you have to send the police for, I was doing nothing wrong, I am really shown up now", said Francis as she stormed yelling into the house, 20 minutes after the call to the Inspector, "this has really pissed me off, I am going to Uni shortly and being treated as a child", she said as she burst into the front room, to see her mother being held by a policewoman, Tom, the Vicar standing by a curtained window and another policewoman bringing in a tray of hot drinks from the kitchen.

"What is happening" screamed Francis as she rushed over to her mother who's still out cold, "Mum, mum, mum" as Francis stroked her hair and face and Judy just lay so still. "What is wrong with Mum" Francis said as she spun around to face Tom. "Francis, I think it best if you sit down, before I answer that", said Tom. Francis did as she was told and sat on one of the chairs not taking her eyes of Tom.

"Your mother has fainted Francis, she has fainted on the tragic news that your Dad has been killed in an accident this evening". Tom never flinched from looking at Francis as he spoke to her and Francis' eyes never left Tom's, but her eyes while still staring began to fill with tears, her hands stoked her chin, came together and became clenched. Still staring at Tom, she asked "what happened?"

"They were all together, your Dad with George Turnbull, Paul Howe and Harry Easton, going to the weekly dart's match, when the car was involved in a shocking incident, all the occupants were killed"

Francis' eyes now left Tom's, her eyes were running, her cheeks were marked by the tear runs, she looked quickly at both police officers and then looked at her mother. "There are some smelling salts in the First Aid box, Dad used so swear by it", her voice stuttered and she repeated "Dad used to swear by it" in the now softer but still stuttering voice. Francis left the room accompanied by Tom, just to see that she was safe. The Ikea First Aid Box was easily found, smelling salts removed, the bottle looked pre-war and probably was.

PC Switski offered to take the salts from Francis, but without a word, Francis indicated "no, she would do this herself". The old bottle was gently opened and Francis, without smelling the salts herself put them near her Mum's nose. Almost immediately Judy coughed and even though her eyes were still shut pushed the small smelling salts bottle away. Judy sat up, her eyes still shut, but still feeling the comfort of somebody on her right. "Mum, it's me, Mum, it's me", pleaded Francis as she grasped her mother's hand, having put the salts away on the coffee table. "Mum, it's me" continued Francis in a very gentle and soft tone, probably the first time she has ever spoken to her mother in such a manner, never having seen her mother in such a vulnerable situation as this before in her life.

Slowly Judy stiffened up as she sat and her eyes, very slowly opened as she continued to cough into her now raised hand. She first saw Frany and offered an empty smile, raising her head further she saw Tom standing by the window, turning to her right saw a policewoman and another standing with a tray in her hand, which she had held since Francis had come home.

"I am at a loss Frany", Judy said as she looked into her daughter's eyes "I am at a total loss, never is my worst nightmare could I imagine losing my John, my love, my life, my heart, my everything", as she spoke her eyes filled and she ended sobbing as Francis, indicated to police officer of her mother's right to move away so she could sit there and hold and comfort each other.

Tom indicated to the police officer with the tray to go to the kitchen and he led the other officer to follow. "They are better left as they are at the moment", said Tom, "I will stay until they are safe with their emotions, you two have done a fantastic job", said Tom as he looked at the faces of both police officers, "thank you so very much" he continued.

With that PC Bloomingdale, picked up her phone and called the Inspector. "PC Bloomingdale here Sir, Mrs Hooper is now awake and being comforted by her daughter and the Vicar is staying for as long as he is needed". "Thanks Francis for the report, if all is in hand you and", he was looking through his papers again "Claire, can head back to the Station and go home for the night, debriefing tomorrow, thanks again and good night". The phone went dead, "that was a man under pressure" commented PC Bloomingdale, "nothing like what the families are going through this Thursday night" responded PC Switski, "so very true" said Tom.

"We'll make our own way out Vicar, I think you could be having a long night" said PC Switski, "such nights are not unusual in my line of work" said Tom with a smile, while offering a hand of friendship to both officers.

The officers left without a further sound and Tom went back into the front room and indicated to Francis that he would sit and stay in the kitchen until they wanted him. Francis gave a thumbs up and Tom went to make a cup strong coffee for himself.

16 FLOUR AND TEARS

Most of the room lights in the bungalow were lit as the police car pulled onto the drive at 9.55 p.m. as requested by the Inspector. On turning off the engine and opening the doors the two officers could hear music and the sound of two women singing their hearts out, it sounded like a party. It was clear the sound was coming from the rear of the property but following protocol they rang the front doorbell.

Amid the sound of the radio and two ladies singing "tie a yellow ribbon…" they just about heard the doorbell. "I'll go" said Georgina, "your much too floury", said a laughing Georgina, as she wiped here her hands-on kitchen towel and took off her apron. Georgina closed the door from the kitchen as she left, to keep the noise down as she approached the front door.

Georgina could see that there were two individuals at that door through the rather large class opaque glass panel in the front door. She opened the door fully to see two rather wet policewomen.

"Mrs Shelley Howe?", enquired the first officer, "Oh no, officer, I am just a friend, Shelley is in the kitchen, is there anything I can do to help?". "May we come in please, it is important and here it is rather wet" said the officer, "so sorry, manners, come in come", said Georgina, "but before we go any further could I see some identification, it is late and I am rather protective of folk?" added Georgina, both officers showed photo-id, which in the light of the hall could have been library cards but Georgina was happy. The first officer identified herself as Vicky Toms and the second as Ann Horne. "Please call us by our first names", said Ann.

The noise was still coming from the kitchen and Shelley could be heard singing another song, but the words and the tune were somehow lost. "May I ask who you are?", said Vicky, "certainly officer, oh sorry Vicky, I am Georgina Wilson, the wife of the Vicar of these parts", said Georgina with a smile and a glance at both officers. "What is this about, should I leave, is it personal to Shelley, what?" "We were told that you were here by your husband", said Ann. "My husband, he is at the Nag's for a darts match, I think you must be mistaken", said Georgina in slightly raised but irritated voice.

"Please, Mrs Wilson, this is not going to be easy", said Ann "and can we talk quietly for the moment" said "Vicky.   "There has been a tragic and fatal accident outside the Nag's tonight.   Four occupants of a car driven by George, Shelley's intended have been killed and that includes Shelley's son Paul". The look of horror on Georgina's face was obvious and for a moment her rather large frame stuttered and swayed. "All dead, no mistakes, all dead?" said Georgina in soft and quiet voice, "All dead" said Vicky.

"Oh my God", said Georgina, putting her back to the wall, with that the kitchen door opened and three in the hall saw Shelley covered in flour, holding an oven tray of tarts still steaming.

"What is happening out there", said Shelly, "am I missing anything, what are the police here for Georgina, paid the parking fine months ago". "Shelley, please clean up a bit and come and sit in the lounge, you need to hear something", said Georgina as she approached Shelley and pointing to the door of the lounge for the officers.

"What is it Georgina, what is it, police always bring bad news don't they", "not always Shelley, but just wash your hands and come through", said Georgina, "shall I make tea", said Shelley as she approached the kettle, "no just leave it for the moment please" said Georgina as she too also cleaned herself further and wondered what on earth to say further. "There is a fresh batch of cakes in the oven" said Shelly, "we should hear the timer in the lounge though" said Shelley as she followed Georgina into the lounge.

The two officers were standing and gestured to Shelley and Georgina to sit down together on the sofa. "My name is PC Vicky Toms; I have shown my ID to Mrs Wilson." "What is all this about", said a confused Shelley. "Please bear with me, it is important what I have to say and it is not easy" said Vicky, while Ann looked on directly at Shelley with tears welling up in her eyes.

Vicky went on "this evening outside the Nag's Head Public House there has been a tragic accident involving a car with 4 occupants and two large lorries", Shelley started looking away from the officers and looking at the floor as if knowing what was coming next, as Georgina's arm came across her shoulder and hugged. "all four occupants of the car were killed in the incident", said Vicky as she opened her notebook and continued. "the car was a purple Ford Mondeo registered to Mr George Turnbull, the occupants of the car, while not having been formally identified include your son Paul Howe". With that Vicky closed her notebook, excused herself, found the downstairs toilet and was sick.

Meanwhile, Shelley just looked to the floor, no movement at all, the only sound was the radio still blaring from the kitchen, Georgina indicated to Ann to turn the radio off and she got the prompt and briefly left. Vicky returned to the lounge just as Ann did.

Shelley raised her eyes and looked straight at Vicky and mouthed "thank you" and then said in a very quiet but clear voice, "what you just had to do, took a very brave person, thank you."

Shelley stood up, looked around her lounge as if it were not at all familiar to her and said, "I need to be on my own, I need to be on my own". Georgina said "I'll stay if you want Shelley, I'll stay", "No" exclaimed Shelley "I want to be on my own, for that is what I now will be and I had better get used to it, such happiness could not be allowed to remain in my life".

Georgina gestured to the officers to leave which they did, both crying and strange for officers, holding each other's hand, as she stood next to Shelley and held her tight, "just go Georgina, I'll see you in the morning, I need to be alone", said a now slightly quivering Shelley as she let go of Georgina's cuddle and sat back down on the sofa.

"I'll go Shelley, I'll turn of the oven on going and see you in the morning" said Georgina as she left the lounge. After coming out of the kitchen, Georgina put on her raincoat and peered back into the lounge to she Shelley still sitting as she was a few minutes ago looking at the floor, with no tears, "God bless you Shelly" said Georgina as she turned to leave, "God bless you Georgina" said an unstirred Shelley.

17 THIS BISH.

One week later, Thursday 4th May.

Tom was on the phone to the Bishop as Georgina walked in with his morning coffee and biscuits to the study.

"................to be quite frank Your Grace, I don't give a monkey's tit, what Saints' day it is next Thursday, the funerals will take place on that day as that is what the families want ....yes Your Grace, barrack room language has no room in the Church, my apologies, but empathy does I believe .... (Tom smiled at Georgina as she put the tray on the desk and he pointed to the chair, indicating that he wanted her to stay) ......no Your Grace, I was not suggesting you lack empathy, it is just that people come before tradition, care comes before process and love come before anything ....yes next Thursday, the 11th of May at 2 p.m. is the funeral, all four will be buried in separate adjacent graves in our Church Yard .... yes we have ample space in our grave yard ....yes the Church Wardens have agreed to this, as has the PCC Secretary (Georgina nodded, she was the PCC Secretary) ....yes, Your Grace the Diocese has been informed as to what we are doing and the necessary procedures and fees will be explained to the families ....no, there is no need for you to come Your Grace, but thank you for the offer, I know the families, so I wish to treat the funeral as a thanksgiving for their lives ....yes I would like two other junior clergy to help with any needs on the day, having to cope with one family at an unexpected death and funeral is hard enough on the emotions but four will be a real stain ....yes I have tried to contact the Rural Dean, but he is on a golfing holiday in Scotland ....yes, two would be good, senior curates ....not three, as my wife can also help, being trained and experienced in bereavement support ....no, Your Grace not Dorothy, Georgina ....your wife has the same name, that is nice ....yes, thank you Your Grace, thank you for your time and understanding, have a lovely day, goodbye.

Tom but the phone down with bang, and uttered "silly old sod, where does the Church find them?"

"There, there" said Georgina, offering Tom a biscuit while he put sugar in the coffee. "Thanks my petal, I don't know what I would do without you", Georgina just smiled, stood up and said, "I'll bring mine through and we can have a chat", "good idea" thought Tom, as Georgina left the study.

Georgina returned, coffee mug in hand and sat opposite Tom at his desk.

Turning to look at the garden, Tom remarked, "why is it regularly raining on a Thursday, or is it just me, look at the stump, it is fair bouncing off, I used to love the rain, now, well, memories".

Tom continued, "before I spoke to the purple duffer, I had the undertakers on the line, all the families are using the same firm so I thought that would make things easier" said Tom mid sips of coffee, "but no, they recon they did not have the resources for four funerals at the same time at the same church", staring at the ceiling and running his hands through what little hair he had left, Tom continued, "and that all changed when I mentioned that the local tv and radio stations have asked for permission to cover the event, suddenly they would pull resources and men from other towns", taking another sip, he looked at a now smiling Georgina and said "folk eh, they are starting to get to me, I should write a book". "By the way Georgie, the tv and radio folk are not being allowed to do their stuff in the church, just the comings and the goings outside on the strict understanding that journalist don't interview the moaners".

"Georgie how is Shelley doing now that some of the family have arrived?" asked Tom with pen and paper to hand.

18 A NEW FAMILY

James Turnbull had got up early this morning and was looking out of the kitchen window on to the garden that his father had so enthusiastically and lovingly looked after. He was watching more than thinking, seeing the rain drops splashing in the bird-bath and bouncing off the garage roof. The water butt was over-flowing from the garage gutter and the grass needed a cut and the beds needed weeding, all observations, no real thought.

He heard a slight sound from the entrance to the kitchen and spun around in surprise, there stood Shelley in her old dressing gown, well-worn slippers, hair everywhere and hands limp at their side. "Your Dad loved that garden James, at times I thought it was his first love" said Shelley turning towards the kettle.

"Would you like a brew, sorry would you like some tea or coffee, I must get used to your North American ways?". "Shelley, I would love a coffee please" said a smiling James as he approached one of the kitchen chairs and sat down. "Your Dad always sat there" said Shelley as she watched James. He moved as if to sit on another chair, "no James, you stay just there, you have at times such a look of your father " said Shelley as she turned to prepare the drinks.

"I'll have this and go and get ready for the day, I don't want to frighten the children with the way I look", said Shelley placing a mug of coffee on the kitchen table, followed by a little jug of milk, a bowl of sugar and a carton of sweeteners. "Thanks Shelley", said James, he continued, "words are not easy at the moment, however I can while we are alone share something very important to me", Shelley looked up from her cup of tea and stared at James, "Dad used to call me regularly, you probably saw from the phone bills and one thing is for sure, in finding you he had not been happier in his whole life and use a comment he made which I treasured he said 'I did not know what love was until I met Shelley', so Shelley I am proud to know you and for the love you shared with Dad", James returned to his coffee and appeared to be looking into the mug as he drank it.

Shelley grabbed a tissue from the box on the kitchen table, they weren't there last Thursday, but now they are all around the house. Dabbing her eyes, "that is probably what makes the hurt all the more, I too found real love and happiness, never ever thinking it was possible again, so thank you for your kind comments, they are more than appreciated". With that and as her voice was failing her, Shelley got up from her chair and left the kitchen, leaving her hardly touch cup of tea.

The dorma-bungalow had three bedrooms, two upstairs in the roof space and one rather large one on the ground floor, Shelley's room was downstairs adjacent to the bathroom. Shelley decided to shower and get herself straight for the day, the family were going for lunch at the Nag's Head, to have something to eat but to also to try to bury the ghosts from that night.

As she returned to her bedroom after the shower, she could hear George's grandchildren playing in the room above, Zoe and Walter, they were far too young to have remembered George, being now 4 and 5 respectively, there fun was just tainted by the general sadness of the adults around them.

Shelley sat at her dressing table and looked in the mirror "what is happening to you girl?", she thought, "time to get the hair right, time to put some colour in your face", with that James shouted through the door, "bathroom free, can I get a shower and shave?", "help yourself James" said Shelley, "I'm trying to put a face on" as she turned and smiled, well tried to smile at herself in the mirror.

Walter came into the kitchen, freshly washed and dressed to see his Dad trying to cook breakfast. "Dad", said Walter, "I don't like having only one bathroom in the house, it is not fair", "sorry Walt, that is the way it is in old houses like this, remember back home this house would be treasured as being ancient, here in England it is just the norm", said James, trying to free bacon, eggs, prepare toast and watch a pan of over boiling beans, "no I am not keen on the old cooking methods either", thought James.

"Walt, if you want juice, it is in the refrigerator", said James still battling with the various pans on the stove. "You can't call that a refrigerator Dad, it is so small", said a small Walt taking a carton of orange juice from the door shelf "and so is the juice box" said an unhappy Walter. "Walt, please stop right now, it is the way here and a refrigerator over here is called a fridge and they like things smaller, get it, please try to be a little more kinder and less negative", James spoke through his teeth, not wanting to raise his voice. Walter sat at table, poured himself a glass of orange juice spilling more on the table than in the glass and just looked at his Dad with a quizzical look.

With that Ann, James' wife, came into the kitchen, her air perfect, slight makeup, a bright summer mostly yellow dress and the requisite slippers. "That smells good", said Ann planting a kiss on James' face, "what a mess Walt, what have you been doing?", Ann said turning to Walter with his orange juice catastrophe, "juice box is too small" said Walter, "I missed the glass". Ann picked up a cloth and wiped up the spillage and finished by wiping Walter with the wet cloth across his nose and smiled.

"Where is Zoe?" said James, starting to dish out his breakfast attempt, "she is in the bathroom" she won't be long said Ann.

Zoe was in Shelley's bedroom; Shelley had dressed and was drying her hair with an electric dryer when Zoe came in. "Can I help Nanna?" said Zoe, "well you can certainly try Zoe", passing the hairbrush to her as she continued with the hair dryer.

A new normality was slowly returning to the house, days after the crash had been horrific for all concerned and the emotions had been stretched to their limits, but now 7 days on a new peace seems to be on Shelley's heart and she was so grateful that James and Ann had been able to change their return flights to 3 days after the funeral and that James' employer had been so supportive in granting extra leave to him.

The family were going to the Nag's Head for lunch, guest of the landlords Gary and Christine.

As they arrived at the Nag's Head, the rain was easing, they could not fail to notice however that the local authority had a cherry-picker out changing the light fitting on the street post, Shelley shuddered.

"Afternoon All", said Gary as they come into the bar. Gary was greeted by a smile from everyone, even Walter. "I have set a table in the restaurant for you, if you wish, but there are no other diners at the moment, or we can set a table round the corner of the bar if you wish. The party all turned to Shelley "I think I would prefer to sit and eat in the bar" said Shelley, "we need to see a little normality please", "no problem at all, take a seat by the fire and I'll get the table sorted", said Gary as he lifted the bar lid and with that Christine his wife appeared, "now what would folk like to drink?"

The meal finished, Zoe and Walter were sat at another table colouring-in, crayons and books provided by the pub. "I don't know what to say, thank you just is not a strong enough word", said Shelley as she looked at both James and Ann sitting opposite her. "Shelley" said Ann, "our emotions have been stretched to their very limits these las few days, but we have come through this with a new 'Mum', in you, the children call you already 'Nanna' and if you don't mind we will drop the Shelley and say 'Mum' in future, both of us", Ann looking briefly at James "didn't have a Mum until you came into our lives through Dad". "I need a drink" said a tearful Shelley "and a strong one at that to toast my new family".

19 CUDDLES
AND SMILES

The sound of laughter from the nursery could be heard clearly in the kitchen while Charlotte and Sam had coffee with some slices of toast and marmalade. "Annemarie and David get on so well together" said Charlotte breaking the morning silence, Sam looked up from staring at her coffee and nodded. "I don't know what to do and I know I have been say that since last Thursday, but I don't know what to do" said Sam still staring at her coffee and totally ignoring the toast.

With that David came rushing towards them both and jumped on to Charlotte's knee closely followed by Annemarie who pushed herself onto Sam's. Both women gave their knee companions a kiss on the head and a cuddle. David reached out for the toast, "not on your life, little man, it will be everywhere" said Sam also restraining Annemarie. "If you now want your breakfast, to your own table you go", said Charlotte, pointing to a scaled down plastic table with two small chairs, fitting the proportions of both. David got down, straight away and followed by Charlotte and sat at their now adopted seats.

"It is amazing how kids adapt" said Charlotte, slicing some toast into soldiers and putting them on plastic plates. "They are better than us, but then we understand the loss, they don't", said a now tearful Sam. "I'll do the toast Sam, you do the drinks", said Charlotte. Sam stopped looking at her coffee and went over to the fridge and poured two plastic beakers half full of milk and took them both to the table, caressing both of their heads in the process.

"Tom is sleeping well, but I guess his long travelling time from Afghanistan has knocked him out", said Charlotte "and his time clock, must be all over the place" added Sam looking towards the hall where some of Thomas's kit lay on the floor. "Mum has confirmed she is coming on Wednesday" said Sam, "she originally suggested about staying in a local B&B, knowing full well I have the room her for her, she just likes to be the centre of the things" continued Sam, "I don't know why she is bothering she never liked Harry, being more concerned about how much he earned than how much of a son-in-law he could be or a father to her grandson, but I have Thomas and you", raising her gaze from her now cooling coffee to look at Annemarie. Sam got off her stool and just hugged Annemarie until both cried and hugged, cried and hugged, with Annemarie very much recalling her own loss and how Sam helped her.

Sam felt a tug on her skirt, looking down from her hug, she saw David, with marmaladed hands looking up so sorrowfully at his Mum. Sam broke from the huddle and picked David up, hugged him and kissed him, David smiled, Sam smiled and said "I love you, my David", "I love you Mum" said David as she put him down, "That is all I want to hear" said Sam.

"Thought I smelt coffee" said Thomas entering the kitchen and wearing a dressing gown he found in the bedroom. "You didn't it is tea", joked Sam, "no you did, sit down, I'll pour you some" said Sam going to the coffee pot. Thomas sat down with the ladies, unshaven for three days, hair a mess, but blue eyes that shone. "Well I haven't seen you Charlotte for years, I heard about your Martin and his accident, I am so sorry my darling", "dark water under the bridge now Thomas, onwards and upwards however life's difficulties present themselves", said Charlotte looking at Thomas' warm blue eyes.

"When is dragon coming over or is she not?" asked Thomas to Sam as she gave him his coffee, "Wednesday", said Sam, "must put the flags out" said Thomas smiling. "What do you want for breakfast Tom?" said Charlotte, "you know what, toast and marmalade looks just fine, with plenty of coffee and I'll be right for whatever you want me to do" responded Thomas, taking a piece of toast from Charlotte's plate with a smile.

"It was only in a mental mist for me yesterday when you arrived Tom, when do you have to return?", "the C.O. has given me two weeks compassionate, counting from the time I left Afghan so I have plenty of time to help assist and generally annoy everyone", smiled Thomas. "I only have to make a few phone calls to arrange my transport back, the Army is good at things like this, poor at many things but not in looking after their own". Thomas continued, "I see it is raining, I haven't seen rain in months, how about I get showered, shaved, it is usually the three s's in the Army, we go for a drive, in the rain, all five of us and find somewhere for a bite to eat, my treat?-", Thomas looked around for some kind of encouraging look, Sam surprisingly looked up first and nodded agreement and smiled followed by Charlotte with the comment "let us get our marmaladed army in the bath Sam, while I make this soldier some more toast". Sam got up, with the first bit of enthusiasm she has expressed for days and gathered up David and Annemarie and led them to the nursery bathroom.

"Not going anywhere else while back in the UK" said Charlotte to Thomas, as she buttered his toast. "No, my sole purpose is to support my big sister, I have nobody in my life except the Army at the moment", said Thomas taking a piece of toast from now Sam's discarded plate.

"All ready?" said Thomas coming down the stairs. His dark brown hair was combed and tidy. His bronzed face more obvious now with the three-day stubble removed. He was dressed in jeans, blue oxford shirt, brown blazer and brown brogues, all not hiding his very fit and slim physique. Charlotte from where she was sat was watching every move as he descended the stairs.

"Sam is ready, she is just finishing getting the kids sorted", said a warm cheeked Charlotte, "you are looking smart Tom", said Charlotte with some emphasis, "why thank you kind lady", smiled Tom taking a bow, "you're not looking bad yourself", "why thank you kind sir", they both laughed, looked at each other for a moment and then looked elsewhere in the large hallway.

"The child-seats are already in the car, so we can go", said Sam coming out of the nursery with both children hand in hand, both looking so smart, clean and tidy, Annemarie in a beautiful pale cream dress, drawn at the waist, matching socks and shoes with a lovely bow in her hair. David in a white rugby shirt, blue shorts and black shoes, looking the perfect angel.

"Charlotte, you look after the children and I'll bring the car round", said Sam grabbing her handbag and taking her raincoat from the hall closet. "OK" said Charlotte as she grabbed two small hands in the hope they would not cause any chaos before the journey. Thomas just sat on one of the hallway chairs and watched the proceedings and then said with a wide smile "I'll drive if I may, it is months since I have driven on a road worthy of the name", "If you can avoid the pot-holes you can" said Sam as she exited the front door.

Charlotte and Thomas never spoke, they exchanged eye contact and smiled and then looked everywhere but at each other, while little hands were still held firm no matter how they tugged and pulled.

The sound of the car was soon heard outside, the canopy outside the front door offered full weather protection to those getting into or out of a car, Harry insisted on it when the house was being designed. So wet weather gear was thrown in the boot and everyone got into the vehicle dry. Sam got out of the car and tossed the keys to Thomas, which he caught cricket fashion, "thanks", he said, as he jumped in the driver's seat. "I'll sit with the children" said Sam, "you sit up front with Tom if you want", with that Charlotte almost flew around the front of the car and jumped into the front passenger seat as Sam struggled getting two reluctant children to be seated and secured in their respective chairs.

"This is some car Sam" said a very impressed Thomas, "where are the whipper controls?", he continued, "everything is automatic, it just happens" said Sam, 'exactly' thought Charlotte.

20 TURNAROUND

"Uncle Stuart, can you do anything to get Mum from her bedroom, she is only leaving it to go to the bathroom and that is it, for nearly a week now, curtains drawn and no conversation, not even when we take her, her meals, I know it is hard, it is hard for all of us with the loss of Dad, but please anything" said Christopher, back from University to support his mother. "I have tried Chris, she looks at me and just turns away with an arm gesture to leave, as she cuddles up to a pillow", he continues "grief is a terrible emotion and folk mourn the loss of a loved one is many and different ways, in a strange way, I have lost a brother and yet my emotional state is being lifted by helping here, if that makes sense", said Paul's brother Stuart over his mug of tea sharing the kitchen table with Christopher also having a morning tea.

"Frany has been stronger than I thought she would be, but again, mourning is a strange process and we should be watchful for her" said Stuart. "I'm having to go back on duty tomorrow, so will be leaving this afternoon, returning on Wednesday as early as I can make it", continued Stuart, "the Force has been very good about leave so no pressure, which is good, I'll be bringing Melly with me, her and Judy have always got on, so I hope she may help on the day and the run up to the day" said Stuart as he rose to pour some more tea.

"By the way where is Frany?" said Stuart looking around, "she normally joins us for morning drinks", "she has gone back to work at the Spar, to hopefully restore some normality to her life", said Christopher.

"The vicar's wife is coming round this morning, I think around eleven, hopefully to bring some life back to Judy, will you be here Chris?" "Yes, Uncle Stuart. I'll be here, nowhere to go, plenty of study books and my own thoughts to deal with", said Christopher while Stuart rose and put a hand on his shoulder, "I may be living up North Chris, but as much as I can, I will be like a rash until Judy is back to being Judy, if that is at all possible", said Stuart as he picked up the morning paper and returned to his chair at the table.

There was knock on the front door, "I'll go" said Stuart, putting down the paper. On opening the door he saw Mrs Wilson, the vicar's wife, with a full shopping bag and dripping rain hood, "come in Mrs Wilson so good to see you again, please come it and get those wet things off" said Stuart offering a hand to take the shopping bag. "Thank you Mr Hooper", said Georgia who added, "please call me Georgia or Georgie, Mrs Wilson is so formal, particularly when Mr Wilson is the vicar", said Georgia with a smile as she looked at Stuart. "Thanks for that Georgia, please call be Stuart, no Scots in the family that I am aware of, but that is what my parents named me", said a smiling but embarrassed Stuart, 'why did I say such rubbish', he thought.

Stuart showed Georgia through to the kitchen where Christopher was seated at the table glancing through the morning paper. "Morning Mrs Wilson" said Christopher, "and a good morning to you Chris and as I have just mentioned to your uncle, please call me Georgia or Georgie, it is less heavier than Mrs", said Georgia with a knowing smile.

"A brew Georgia?", said Christopher, "the pot is still fresh", "yes please" said Georgia as she sat down at the table and was joined by Stuart, the pair just looked at one another as Georgina awaited he tea, which arrived steaming, "milk?" said Christopher, "yes please Chris, but no sugar, must look after what figure I have got left", Georgina said with a smile.

"Now that we are together and before I go and see Judy I think it best that I describe where I and the vicar think we are with the arrangements for next Thursday", said Georgian digging in her shopping bag and producing a note book and pencil. "Oh I forgot, I have been baking, the bag is full of fattening things for the family, naughty but nice, well I hope they are" said Georgina, seeing nodding smiles from both Christopher and Stuart.

"So if I may, I will read from my notes and just jump in if there is anything you don't understand or disagree with, I hope none of the latter though", she said with a smile to each face looking at her. "The funerals will take place at two in the afternoon, next Thursday in St Mary's Church and the burials will take place in the Church yard immediately after the funeral service. As agreed with all families, it will be a joint funeral, all four coffins will be in Church together, a member of each family or close friend will be invited to speak and a pieces of music special to each family will be played during the service, either from a CD, tape or by the organist, recorded music would be better, the organist is getting on a bit" said Georgina smiling and looking at both Chris and Stuart. "So I need tomorrow, at the latest, the name of the nominated family member or friend to speak, we need this for the order of service as we do a suitable piece of music, so who can do this?" said Georgian looking around, "It will have to be me" said Chris, "yes that is right" said Stuart "I must report for duty tomorrow, back on Wednesday" he continued. "Good" said Georgina "please don't let me down, I have the information from the other families, I am just aware on how much more difficult it is here with Judy, so please tomorrow". She continued "all the coffins are identical except for the name plates and if you want any special inscription on the plate, please let the undertakers know by Saturday at the very latest. A funeral car for the immediate family, it will take 6, will arrive here at one thirty, the hearse will be in front of the car and will process from here to the Church. All four hearses will be arriving at roughly the same time so everything will be a little slow but the dignity of the occasion will we hope be preserved as best as possible, all good so far?" said Georgina looking around the table and getting a nod of approval

"Normally all this would be told my the undertaker, which it has to the other families, however with Judy being temporarily out of it, we need to do it this way, I am doing my best", said Georgia, "you certainly are", said an appreciative Stuart, "the service will be longer than a normal funeral service as clearly more than normal is happening, that is fine, it is just important that the wishes of the families, that the men have their send off together are respected and honoured. You will be pleased to know that, while my husband is obliged to offer a sermon, it will be short.

Now this is important, the accident created a good deal of media interest and the local radio and tv have intimated that they may attend the service", said Georgia, as she was stopped with a "no" from Christopher, "no, my father's funeral is not a circus, no I am not happy" continued Chris now standing up. "Chris, you have not allowed me to finish what I was saying, please sit down", said Georgina. "We cannot stop the radio and tv people from reporting on the arrivals and leavers of the service, however, my husband the vicar, has come to an arrangement with them, they may, without being intrusive, be on Church property, they are not to enter the Church building under any circumstances and they are not, repeat not, to attempt to interview any of the moaners", said Georgina turning to Chris, "does that do it?", "I think so said Chris, "sorry", Christopher added, "no need to apologise, I totally agree with you, I just hope they honour our agreement" said Georgina. "The police will also be in attendance to ensure parking and traffic movements are safe, Inspector Forbes who was on duty on that night of nights will be supervising and he has asked if the families mind if the constables who attended the families on the night of accident attend the service" said Georgina turning to Stuart. "I have absolutely no objection" said Stuart, "Nor I" added Chris, "that is good" said Georgina "the other families are also in agreement".

"We now come to the internment, the burial proper, the men will be buried in turn with the formal words of internment and ceremony spoken at each grave, this will add significantly to the total time, however it is important that we undertake this with greatest respect possible to the living as well as the deceased. The burials will take place in alphabetical order, starting with Harry Easton, then your Dad", said Georgina looking at Chris, "followed by Paul Howe and then George Turnbull, all should be over by about three thirty and families if they wish can stay in Church until the time of their loved one's internment starts, the undertakers will take each coffin in turn to the grave side". Georgina continues "to be practical, it makes sense if only close family and dear friends are at the grave side, I hope you can help us there?" "I agree" said Stuart "too many folk around the various open graves could be a real issue" he added.

I don't know if you are aware of this but the landlords of the Plough and the Nag's Head are jointly arranging the Wake, providing all the food, but not a free bar, which will be held at the Plough, for obvious reasons". "What a lovely gesture", said Stuart, "I hadn't even thought about the afters" continued Stuart, "nor me" said Christopher, "I think you had other things to deal with" added Georgina. "Fortunately, the 'back room' as they call it can accommodate a large number of people in its licence so numbers will not be a problem" said Georgina.

"I'll go and see Judy now and if there is anything that is not clear or you want changing, not happy with let me know when I come down" said Georgina as she took various containers from her shopping bag and placed them on the kitchen worktop, before heading for the stairs.

"What a woman" said Stuart, "without the help of her and others in this almighty mess, we would still be in it" he added, "I don't often cry Uncle, but reality of what is happening to me and my family is hitting home and I do not like it" said Chris whipping his eyes with the sleeve of his jumper.

"Uncle Stuart, it is Chris", "what time do you call this?", "sorry, you promised to call when you got home and didn't" said Chris impatiently, "sorry yes I did, sorry I am home and in bed" said a blunt Stuart, "you have to know, mum is back to being mum, I don't know what the vicar's wife said or did, but mum showered, got dressed came down and made tea and spoke to us both rationally, emotionally and when we explained everything that was to happen next week, she cried a little and just said thank you" said a very happy Christopher.

"Chris I am so very happy, I'll get Melly to call your mum tomorrow, sleep well young man and thanks for calling and apologies for being initially grumpy" said Stuart and then hanging up.

21 BABY

The picture was idyllic, Toni's mother, was sitting on the couch, wearing her dressing gown, in the conservatory. looking over a wet dawn, brightened by a new sun, dark clouds on the horizon and feeding her 6-day old granddaughter Phoebe (Phoebe Pauline Irene Howe). "Phoebe certainly likes her bottle" said Grandmother Irene to her daughter Toni, bringing in two cups of coffee and some warm crumpets and placing them on the small table in front of the couch. "Yes, she does, pity it has to be at 5.30 a.m. in the morning" replied Toni.

"How are you feeling today, love?" said Irene, having taken her first drink of the day. "Still sore Mum, still in a daze, still lost, still empty and yet overwhelmed by having such a beautiful Phoebe" said Toni as she reached over and stroked the baby's head, who made no movement except to continue to suck on the bottle with eyes shut.

"I know you were getting agitated, but really everything is under control. The vicar has been amazing, Bob is running the shop as normal and his wife Sharon has stepped in with the deliveries and the family solicitors and Paul's accountant are working together to get everything sorted". "Probate?" said Irene, "Mum I know nothing about Probate, Paul did leave a will so it is all being dealt with properly, I now need to concentrate on ensuring the Jack and Phoebe are OK and have a normal as possible life", "I'll help anyway I can" said Irene, looking down at the baby, "I'm counting on it Mum" said a now smiling Sam as Tom came into the conservatory with his favourite ball, hoping for a play.

"I'll let him out through the conservatory doors, he hates rain, so he will not be long", said Toni walking to the door with Tom behind, ball still in mouth. "There you go boy", said Toni, ball dropped on floor Tom shoots out of the door stops, hurries to a dry area of the patio, has a wee and shoots back all in 15 seconds, "see I said he didn't like the rain, normally he would roam the garden for hours, but not when it is wet", said Toni as he closed the door on Tom's return.

"Mum, if you don't mind, I am going back to bed", said Toni running her hands through her hair, "You go love, I'm more than happy, doing what grannies do, don't forget your coffee" said Irene, "I'll leave it, I want to sleep, oh do I want to sleep" said Sam, "if the house remains quiet" said Toni looking at Tom, chewing on his ball, "Jack will sleep for hours yet", "off you go", said Irene as she was kissed by Toni, with a "thanks Mum" followed by a another kiss on Phoebe's head, "Never thought something so beautiful could come out of so much darkness" said Toni as she walked away with tears welling up again.

Jack was having his lunch of beans and burgers, "he loves them", said Toni as she prepared omelettes for her Mum and herself, "whatever", said a clearly disagreeing grannie. "Surprising that Jack has not mentioned Paul at all, not asked where he is, is he coming home, it is like the boy has closed the door on him", said Toni in whispers to her Mum, "for the best, I guess, or perhaps he senses your loss and does not want to cause further hurt, we will neve know, he is so young", said Irene still happily nursing Phoebe.

Jack was nearly finished as two omelettes were placed on the table by Toni, "shall I put Phoebe in the crib while we eat Mum" said Toni, "not on your life" retorted Irene, she stays here, I used to nurse you like this, while eating, we didn't have cribs in those days and your Dad, God Bless him, was broadly useless in such matters" said a smiling Irene. Irene had one of those smiles that was infectious and could warm a room, that simple expression meant so much to Toni and reminded her of past times.

"Jack has afternoon pre-school at two, I have spoken to the nursery, they know why he has not been attending, but things must get back to normal, well as normal as they can", said a busy Toni as she cleared the plates away and then led Jack to the downstairs bathroom to get all the bean sauce off his face, hands and elsewhere.

"Well, that is Jack, bathed and put to bed, tucked in and he fell asleep almost immediately, I just wonder what goes through the little chaps mind", said Toni as she entered the lounge and seeing her Mum still nursing Phoebe, who as usual was still asleep. "Nearly time for her last but one feed of the day" said Irene, "OK, I get the hint" said Toni, with a smile "I'll do the bottle if you do the bum", said Toni returning to the kitchen while Irene, Phoebe in her arms progressed to the nursery, "by, she is a bit pongy" said Irene wrinkling her nose, which nobody else could see.

"What is on telly?" said Irene, as the three of them sat on the sofa in the lounge, Phoebe in her nanny's arms and Toni cuddling up to Tom. "I haven't got a clue Mum, here's the remote control it's yours, I am just getting some kind of happiness back after the hell of the last few days" said Toni, "pass me my glasses will you Toni, I cannot see the buttons properly on this remote, why do they make them so small?" said Irene, "any whisky left?" she added.

22 THURSDAY AND IT'S RAINING

St Mary's Church is the old parish Church of Sprockly dating from the 14th Century. It is sited on the main square of the town, with a war memorial in the centre and directly opposite the Plough Inn which is next to a branch of Boots the Chemist. Various other shops, cafes, banks and offices surround the square, but St Mary's is the big architectural and historical feature. The vicarage, is behind the Church building linked by a short path which borders the graveyard, which covers about an acre of land, this is very well kept by a local farmer who brings his sheep to graze on the grass, not very good for any flowers but the graveyard's grass is like a manicured lawn.

The police had been out early morning putting no-parking cones in areas were previously anyone could park and a local BBC TV truck, had parked up, complete with a satellite dish on its roof. The usual flower tubs and hanging baskets were all around the square and from light standards, getting well-watered by the constant drizzle, which looked set in for the day.

Judy Hooper was sat at her kitchen table having a final coffee before the car was due to arrive, "Mum you look amazing", said her son Christopher, who had just walked into the room, Judy looking up smiled warmly, "Chris so do you, I have not seen you in a proper suit for years, you look very handsome, your Dad will be proud", said a proud mother. "I had to go out and get this M&S's best, but when did you get the dress, you didn't go out?" enquired

Chris, "I bought it a few months ago, for Shelley and George's wedding, your Dad loved it, I love it and I am wearing the wedding clothes as are most of the ladies today for we have agreed that today of all days will be bright and we shall wear what we would have worn at the wedding and that includes Shelley" said a smiling Judy, checking her makeup in her handbag mirror "Wow" said Christopher, as Francis came in looking equally amazing but with tearful

eyes and spoilt makeup, "Mum, I having real difficulty with this, I have to do it for Dad, you, Chris and everyone else, but I cannot appear to do it for myself" said a now crying Francis. "Come here my doll", said Judy standing up and moving over to Francis, "Don't make me cry", said Judy "my tear ducts are worn out" she added, she saw a glimmer of a smile on Francis' face, sit down here, we have fifteen minutes before the car is due and let me help with the makeup and Chris can go and see what Uncle Stuart and Melly are doing.

Just as Chris opened the kitchen door to the hall Stuart and his wife, Melly came into the kitchen. "My, we are all looking smart this afternoon, Judy you look amazing, Frany very much the young woman and Chris, well, you handsome fellow", said Stuart as he gave Chris a big hug, Melly smiled a kind of shy smile and said nothing.

"Have you got everything you need Tom", said Georgina, as she put his freshly pressed surplice in his suit bag along with his cassock, "yes, everything", said Tom, "got my sermon, the order of service and the most important thing for today, an umbrella" said a smiling Tom as he kissed Georgina, "see you at the Church Georgie" said Tom, kissing Georgina, as he headed for the front door of the vicarage and for his short walk to the Church.

Toni was busy getting Jack washed and dressed while Irene was changing Phoebe and getting her into a new dress bought for the occasion. 'I love the smell of babies after they have been bathed, oiled and powdered, nothing like it' thought Irene as she lifted

Phoebe up and laid her in the carry cot. As soon as she was down, Phoebe rooted for a dummy, found her mouth and sucked away, oblivious to the loving eyes of her grandmother and how she was been tucked in. Toni came down with Jack, "You look lovely my dear, lovely enough to be going to a wedding and Jack you look very much the young man" said a proud Grandmother, "you're not looking to bad either for a granny", smiled Toni, "car will be here in about 10 minutes, have we got everything?" said Irene.

Thomas finished his phone call with "thank you Sir, see you in a week or so". Turning to his sister Sam, he said "It is OK for me to wear uniform at the wedding, so your wish is my command my sister", as he bowed to his very beautifully dressed sister. "You had better hurry" said Sam "the car is due in 10 minutes", "don't worry" he replied bounding up the stairs, "I have all my clothes laid out in the bedroom", with that sound of his bedroom door closing made a louder than normal noise. Sam looked around the house from her position in the hallway and saw that she had everything but felt so empty. Further noise was heard upstairs as Charlotte, with both David and Annemarie came down the stairs. Sam clapped her hands on seeing the two children, looking so beautifully smart. Sam held out her hands and grasped both David and Annemarie hands and she knelt down in front of them, "I am relying on you both to be more than good while we are in Church, there will be time after to have fun, but please be good and you must be strong for me", see looked at David "today David we are saying a final goodbye to your Daddy", tears formed in her eyes so she looked away, "I want you to be really strong for me, you will sit next to me and I want you to hold me hand throughout the time we are in Church, is that OK?", David looked up and pulled his hand so Sam went close and he kissed his mum.

Shelley was having a real problem with the hat pin, she kept sticking it into her head, "shall I help", said Ann, "I'm ready and James is getting Zoe and Walter smartened up". "Thanks Ann, it is appreciated" said Shelley as Ann pricked her finger with the hat pin, "never used these before and I don't think I ever will again" said Ann with a smile, looking at Shelley through the reflection from the dressing table mirror. "Your outfit is amazing" said Ann, "I bought it for George, but he would not have cared if we had married in overalls and wellies" said a smiling Shelley. The pin went in, no screams of pain, the hat is firmly on the head, the car arrives in 5 minutes.

The Church Organist was playing one of those pieces of music that only church organists play as the first hearse arrived outside the Church, just as the drizzle that had been on all day eased. Orders of Service had been placed on all the pews, more pages than normal, but then this was no normal funeral. The Church was a mass of colour, Harry's company had insisted on providing the flowers and there was no expense spared. The variety of flowers was amazing, the arrangements spectacular without any fragrance so as not to upset those with hay fever problems. As the drizzle eased so the sun started to shine and coming through the west window it lit the front of the Church from the Chancel steps to the east end. The local police had done an amazing job, ensuring that there was just enough space in front of the Church for a hearse to remove the coffin and to accommodate a funeral car.

The first hearse was for George, followed by the car holding Shelley, James, Ann and the children Zoe and Walter. The undertakers removed the coffin from the hearse, in their well drilled but respectful manner, onto a well chromed gleaming trolley and waited until those in the car were behind them and processed into the Church. As soon as they processed, the vehicles moved away for the next to arrive. All being watched by a big crowd of on-lookers and TV cameras.

Shelley entered the Church to find it virtually full except for the front four pews, two on the right and two on the left. Heads turned to watch them enter the Church, Shelley recognised some, but not all, she caught the eye of Vicky and Ann the two police officers who brought the news and they exchanged brief nods and discreet smiles of acknowledgement. The trolley holding the coffin of George was stopped and made secure to the left of the Chancel steps, so Shelley and party took their places in the front pew on the left. As soon as they were seated Tom, the vicar came over and said a few words, just as the second coffin was being brought in.

Paul Howe's coffin was stopped and braked next to George's and the Howe family were immediately behind Shelley's. Shelley's shoulder was tapped by Toni, she turned round and was given a loving kiss and hug from her daughter-in-law as she looked over beaming with a smile at Phoebe (her granddaughter) sleeping so soundly in the carrycot. Tom came over to Toni and had a few words of comfort and Irene and Shelley mouthed together at each other, "see you later", "see you later".

John's was the next coffin brought into Church, the organist was still playing what organists play and this was stopped and parked to the right of the Chancel steps. Judy was looking around at such a packed Church, just looking for one face and found it, Georgina was sat on the right of the Church in the third pew, they both smiled and Georgina gave Judy a knowing nod. Once seated Tom came over to speak to speak to Judy and gave her a kiss.

The final coffin was Harry's, it was stopped and braked next to John's and the family took their places in the second pew on the right behind John's family. Sam holding tightly to David's hand, as Charlotte was doing to James, looking very smart indeed in his uniform and hardly taking her eyes off him. Tom spoke briefly to Sam, Charlotte kept hold of James' hand. Sam had one of those strange feelings and just had to stand and turnaround, amongst the hundred or so folk in Church her eyes found her mother's who she had not spoken to for years, Mum smiled, Sam didn't, she just turned and sat down again.
The organist finished, much to the relief of most in the congregation, as Tom took his place at the dais.

"Good afternoon" Tom started, "we are gathered here to give thanks for the lives of Harry Easton, John Hooper, Paul Howe and

George Turnbull", he looked at each coffin in turn as he spoke.

Tom continued "Let us pray ...."

"I would like to invite Thomas, Harry's brother-in-law to say a few words" said Tom as he took his seat behind the dais.

Thomas rose, Charlotte letting go of his hand and he progressed to the dais with notes in hand. Thomas stood their soldier erect, with his pristine uniform and buttons gleaming in the bright sunlight coming from the west window. "Harry was a special man" he started "a man of the City and all its pressures and privileges but a man who loved the life of being here in Sprockly. He loved his family and he adored his cars, oh his cars .... to conclude, we were asked to pick a piece of music that was appropriate to Harry's life, well Harry loved the Beatles, so the song 'Baby you can drive my car' is most appropriate as he didn't like anyone to drive his prized collection including Sam", he concluded with a smile to Sam and as he came down the steps he tapped on Harry's coffin, sat down and Charlotte gathered his hand and they both exchanged knowing smiles.

Tom approached the dais "well I have not heard that one for a while, thank you Harry and for what you do for our country and now I would like to invite Stuart, John Hooper's brother to speak".

Stuart stood up and kissed Judy as he passed her in the pew and proceeded to the dais taking his notes from his jacket pocket. "It can honestly be said, I have known Paul, all my life, all my life", Stuart's voice broke and he held the dais for support, he continued "life can be so cruel and yet with the memories it can also be special and beautiful, as a brother .... now the family have thought a good deal of what music to play and given John's love of tinkering we thought a song my Mike and the Mechanics would be appropriate and chose the 'Living years' for today the lyrics are more than appropriate, thank you"

The music started as Stuart left the dais and like Thomas, he tapped John's coffin with his hand.

Tom getting back to the dais was clearly moved by the music and stood there for a moment reviewing the faces in the congregation, many now crying or drying an eye.

"I would now like to invite Toni, the wife of Paul's wife to say a few words"

Toni got up and approached the dais, what sounds there were in the Church prior to this, were no more, the building was so silent as she climbed the few stairs of the Chancel and approached the dais. She carried no notes.

"Nobody wants to go through what we have gone through" said Toni as she made a sweeping movement of her hand towards the front pews, looking at all the families. "We have been to hell and back and found peace from I don't know where, my Paul was my Paul, yes we had our ups and downs .... love, as we enjoyed it is eternal, I will cherish", her voice now broke "I will cherish him, his memory for the rest of my life, thank you Paul, thank you, thank you". Toni looked down and saw that Shelley was sobbing and left the dais to go down to comfort her. From back sprung a start of applause that cascaded through the Church.

Tom getting back to his dais and looking at the now seated Toni said "I have seen many brave things in my life Toni, but your words have been inspirational, moving and from the heart, so on behalf of all here thank you", Tom continued, I'll introduce the music, Toni told me why this was chosen, probably the first time ever played at a funeral service , the theme tune to Dad's Army, Paul loved the programme particularly, particularly Corporal Jones the Butcher, Paul's profession.

Phoebe started to cry, so before any further proceedings, Georgina went over to Irene and suggested she took the baby into the Vestry so that she could stay for the rest of the service. Irene passed over the carrycot and a baby-bag with all the necessary for bum and mouth smiled gratefully to Georgina.

"And now", said Tom, at his dais, "I would like to invite James Turnbull, son of George to say a few words".

When James got to the dais, he rummaged in his pockets for his notes, not finding them, he said "Oops, it looks like I am without notes in support, so here goes, my dad George, his cap was famous, when we were young we thought he slept in it, I know he bought new ones but they always looked years old within days .... in Shelley he found a love like he had never experienced before, how do I know, he told me so and a man would not say such things to another man unless the words were bound in absolute truth, thanks Dad, may you rest in peace with your cap. Thank you. Oh, nearly forgot the music, Dad liked his country music and as I mentioned he loved his garden, so it must be "Rose Garden".

James left the dais and kissed his dad's coffin as he returned to his seat.

Tom at his dais started "I'll keep this short, for we have heard many great tributes to these men and we celebrate their lives, what they have brought to the world, the memories that they leave and the fellowship that bonded them. St Paul said in .... and the greatest of them is love, Amen.

"That concludes the Church service, the families invite you to join them in the Plough afterwards for Afternoon Tea, well in the Plough there will also be other beverages". The next part of the proceedings is for close family and nominated friends as lay our day friends to rest in our churchyard. We must keep the numbers down owing to the dangers of four open graves and wet grass, so please respect the families wishes. Thank you" said Tom as he gave the organist the nod to play what organists play and the churchwarden opened the big doors at the west end of the Church which let in even more light. Other clergy in the congregation invited those who were not to attend the burials to quietly leave the Church. Within a few minutes most of the Church was empty except for the front pews and a solitary lady at the back a Mrs

Susan Kempt, Sam's mother.

The undertakers came forward and took up Harry Easton's coffin on their shoulders and proceeded to go through the north door towards the graveyard followed by his family, just as she got to the door, Sam stopped and waved at her mother to join her. The service at the graveside followed the Church of England rite, flowers were thrown on the coffin as it was laid and the party left to go to the Plough, Tom did this another three times and all went as best it can in such circumstances.

Meanwhile, outside the Church there were big crowds watching, for what you have to wonder, the journalists filmed part of the burials without intrusion as they had promised, but one nearly got flattened by Thomas as they approached Sam who was being supported by a rediscovered mother, only being restrained by a very attentive Charlotte.

23 THE END DO

The Plough was already busy when the first funeral party arrived, four tables had been reserved for the families. As soon as Sam saw them, she asked for them to be somehow put together "we have said goodbye to our men, together we will have their wake together please" said Sam.

Many greetings, many smiles, many old tales were told amongst the sandwiches, sausage rolls, pork pies, cheese and onion on sticks, pizza slices, chicken wings, etc, etc.

"Did you enjoy that?" asked Tom as Georgina arrived back at the Vicarage, "looking after the baby, you bet I did, she smelt a bit, but then so do you after curry" Georgina said with a smile, "we going over to the Plough? asked Georgina, "in a while Georgie, in a bit", Tom said as he went outside through the conservatory door towards the tree stump.

Georgina watched him, still in his cassock, Tom just leaned over the stump, perhaps for a few minutes, stood up and came back in. "The stump is wet again Georgie, wet again", "Its not raining Tom", "no it's not, but with tears, Georgie, with tears", with that he hugged Georgina and sobbed, she suddenly thought what emotions my man has to hold in, it is good for him to cry, she kissed his forehead and they hugged for a while. "Right" he said, "enough of that I need a pint, off to the Plough".

Printed in Great Britain
by Amazon

46727700R00084